BUFFY HEARD A LOW GROWL.

It sounded way too close and too loud—in fact, it almost whispered in her ear. She heard long jaws click together, and she knew a beast was right behind her, ready to attack. Buffy whirled around and lifted her hand to ward off the attack, but it didn't come—at least not at that instant.

The wise old hunter was too crafty to take her on all by himself. He lifted his snout and howled in a chilling tone that sounded like Mom calling the kids to dinncr. When he was answered by excited yipping, Buffy bounded to her feet and looked for an escape route.

There was none. In every direction, all she saw were wild-eyed, snarling coyotes charging toward her. . . .

Buffy, the Vampire Slayer™

Buffy, the Vampire Slayer (movie tie-in)
The Harvest
Halloween Rain
Coyote Moon
Night of the Living Rerun
The Angel Chronicles, Vol. 1
Blooded
The Angel Chronicles, Vol. 2

Available from ARCHWAY Paperbacks

Buffy the Vampire Slayer adult books

Child of the Hunt
Return to Chaos

Available from POCKET BOOKS

COYOTE MOON

John Vornholt

Based on the hit TV series created by Joss Whedon

AN ARCHWAY PAPERBACK
Published by POCKET BOOKS
New York London Toronto Sydney Tokyo Singapore

This book is a work of fiction. Names, characters, places and incidents are products of the author's imagination or are used fictitiously. Any resemblance to actual events or locales or persons, living or dead, is entirely coincidental.

AN ARCHWAY PAPERBACK *Original*

An Archway Paperback published by
POCKET BOOKS, a division of Simon & Schuster Inc.
1230 Avenue of the Americas, New York, NY 10020

ISBN: 0-671-01714-4

First Archway Paperback printing January 1998

10 9 8 7 6 5 4

Printed in the U.S.A.

IL: 7+

To my researchers,
Nancy, Sarah, and Eric Vornholt,
and Lee Whiteside

COYOTE MOON

Chapter 1

The night wind brought a howl that was sharp and high-pitched, like a baby crying. Only it wasn't a human baby. Buffy Summers paused to listen as she stepped out of the Bronze, Sunnydale's coolest club. Of course, it was Sunnydale's *only* club, and they let everybody in—but it was still cool, somehow.

The door opened again, and Xander, her friend, stepped into the dark alley, bumping into her with his gangly body. "Hey, Buffy, this is a doorway, not a parking lot."

"Sorry," she said. "Do you hear that?"

Xander frowned as he listened to the rock music thumping through the walls. "Do you think the band finally hit the right chord?"

"No way," Buffy answered. "It was something else, like a howl."

The door opened again, and Willow stepped out

and bumped into them. "Are we pretending to be the Three Stooges?" she asked.

"No," Xander answered. "That's when we all try to go through the door at the same time. This is where we stand in the alley and listen to . . . What are we listening to?"

Buffy shook her mane of honey-blond hair. "I don't know, just some weird sound—like a howl."

"Are you sure it wasn't the lead singer?" Willow asked.

Buffy sighed. "Okay, so tonight wasn't Lollapalooza at the Bronze. Have you got a better idea where to go?"

"We could go home and sleep?" Willow said hopefully.

"There's plenty of time to sleep once school starts again," Xander scoffed. "Biology, English literature, study hall in the library—what could be more restful? But for right now, we've got to *party!*"

"He's right," Buffy insisted. "The break's almost over, and it's our duty as teenagers to have as much fun as possible before school starts."

Willow looked wistful. "I think school's more fun than vacation."

"That's why we hang with you," Xander said. "You're really bizarre."

Buffy started walking down the service road that cut between the warehouses around the Bronze. "During those desperate times when there's no party anywhere else, I know two guys who never let you down—Ben and Jerry! My mom just put in a supply of cookie dough ice cream."

"My favorite!" Xander claimed.

With Buffy the Vampire Slayer leading the way, the three friends wandered from the bad part of town, across the tracks, onto a well-lit suburban street. Buffy had to admit that things had been a bit boring lately—what with no school plus no vampires to slay—but she wasn't going to complain. Vampire vacation was even better than school vacation.

"Listen," Willow said excitedly. "I just heard there's a carnival opening this weekend in the vacant lot on Main Street, where the drive-in movie used to be!"

"What kind of carnival?" Xander asked.

"You know," Willow said, "a cheap, tawdry affair with creaky rides and hokey fun houses."

"Cool!" Xander exclaimed. "Just the thing we need to end the break."

"And blow all the money we made from babysitting," Buffy added.

Enthused about the coming weekend, the three teenagers walked more quickly past the grassy lawns and sedate houses. Except for the way it looked, there was nothing sedate about the town of Sunnydale. It was perched on the Hellmouth, a very special place where the forces of darkness converged and attracted monsters from all over the world. *Real* monsters.

As they walked under a street lamp, Buffy turned

and saw a smudge under Xander's lip. She licked her finger and started to wipe it off. "Hold still, Xander, there's chocolate milkshake on your lip."

He smiled sheepishly and pushed her hand away. "Uh, that's my new goatee. I've got that whole Skeet Ulrich–Johnny Depp thing going."

Willow grinned but quickly covered her mouth. "Oh, it's very dashing."

Xander beamed proudly. "Do you think so?"

"If you want a mustache," Buffy said, "I think you'd better grow the hair in your nose longer."

"That stinks," Xander complained, slouching ahead of the girls. "I'll probably shave it off, but you could let me enjoy it until school starts, okay?"

"Okay," Buffy said with amusement. "Don't wig out."

Willow frowned puzzledly at her. "Why do men want to grow hair on their faces?"

"They're primitive," Buffy said with a shrug. "Deep down, under all that deodorant and after-shave, most of them would like to sleep in a cave and pick bugs out of their hairy hides."

"But Xander is more refined," Willow said with a hopeful lilt to her voice. "He wouldn't really grow a bunch of facial hair, would he? I'm scared of things that are *too* hairy."

Buffy twitched as the fine hairs on the back of her neck stood on end—they must not have liked Willow's remark. She also felt a slight cramp, reminding her of the next full moon. But she couldn't think about that now, because the hairs on her neck continued their edgy dance.

She knew they were in grave danger. *But from where? From what?* Instinctively she slowed her pace and went into a crouch.

Suddenly a pack of wild animals burst from one of the side yards and loped to a stop in front of Xander. With a startled howl, the mustachioed hero sprang backward and scurried toward Buffy. While her friends fell in line behind the Slayer, the pack completed a lazy circle around them. Their actions reminded Buffy of a pack of hyenas she had once encountered at the zoo, but they looked more like dogs.

Then the Slayer realized what the predators were—*coyotes.*

She had seen coyotes often in the hills around Los Angeles, where she used to live, while horseback riding in Griffith Park or walking near Dodger Stadium. But that was always from a distance—she had never seen a pack of coyotes at close quarters, and it was a startling experience.

Numbering about fifteen, they were a scrawny, scruffy bunch, with mangy coats and darting eyes. Their tongues hung languidly over long jaws and jagged teeth, and they panted as if they had run a long distance. In their wary eyes, Buffy saw mischief and intelligence. She knew she should stay on her guard, but it was hard to be afraid of them when they looked so much like dogs. *Well, maybe dogs that need a bath and a trim. And a decent mud pack,* she thought.

None of them would meet her gaze except for one—an old gray coyote with rheumy, yellow eyes. It stopped and stared at her with a wisdom that seemed to be ancient.

To cover his initial fright, Xander swaggered toward the scrawny predators. "Hey, man, it's just coyotes. Shoo! Go away!"

Some of the scruffy beasts did back away a few steps, but others bared their long canine teeth.

"Xander, leave them alone," Buffy ordered, still in her fighting stance. "Don't start any trouble."

"Oh, come on, they're just coyotes. You're new here, but we see them all the time."

"Duh," Buffy said testily. "I saw coyotes in Los Angeles all the time, too. This bunch *looks* normal, but there's something wiggins about them."

Even Willow scoffed at her fear. "He's right, Buffy. It's unusual to see them this close, but coyotes come down from the hills this time of year, looking for water."

As if on some silent command, the pack of coyotes whirled gracefully on their haunches and loped away. Their joyous, high-pitched yips sounded like a bunch of marauding bandits in an old John Wayne movie. Within seconds, most of them had disappeared around a corner.

"See, they're chicken!" Xander claimed, proudly puffing out his chest. He shouted after the coyotes, "Yeah, go on! Get out of here!"

The old coyote with the weird eyes stopped at the corner to look back at Buffy, and she felt the cramps, the chills, the heaves, and just about every other warning sign her body was capable of producing. The animal didn't look annoyed—just curious. Finally it dashed off after its buds, and their eerie yipping continued to pierce the night for many minutes.

"They're on the hunt," Willow said cheerfully. "I did a report on coyotes in zoology, so I know about their habits."

"Don't you think there's something way bizarre about them?" Buffy asked. "Apart from the fact that coyotes are bizarre, anyway."

"No," Willow answered thoughtfully. "But coyotes *are* strange. Did you know, you can train bears, tigers, elephants, and just about every other creature on earth—but not coyotes. In the wild or in captivity, coyotes do their own thing. Native Americans have all kinds of tales about them."

"They're just dumb dogs," Xander said, grinning at Buffy. He put his arm protectively around her shoulders. "Don't worry, Buff. If you're scared of those big bow-wows, I'll protect you."

She shook off his gangly arm. "That's real Hercules of you, but as long as they stay away from us, we'll have no problem."

"Xander is right," Willow said reassuringly. "We see them around here a lot. Even though coyotes live all over the West, often near urban areas, it's very rare for them to attack humans."

"I'll remember that." Buffy gave her wispy friend a smile. She didn't want to get mad at Xander and Willow; after all, it wasn't often they got to act more macho than the Slayer. Maybe it was just a pack of especially bold coyotes, new in town, razzing the locals. Still, she couldn't get the aged eyes of that grizzled coyote out of her mind.

With her heightened senses, Buffy could still hear the coyotes as they continued their romp through Sunnydale's quiet streets. Their depraved yowls sounded like a combination of tomcats, wolves, and two-year-old toddlers. Buffy was glad when the awful yelps faded into the starlit distance.

"The children of the night," Xander said in his best Bela Lugosi imitation. "What beautiful music they make."

"You know, he always gave me the creeps," Buffy said, "because I don't think he knew what he was saying. He, like, learned it phonetically. And why did he walk around with his cape in front of his mouth? Did he have bad breath? All the vampires I know like to have their fangs hanging out, primed and ready."

"I'm going to pass on ice cream," Willow said with a yawn. "It's time to go home—to dream of returning to school and ending this pointless existence."

"It's called *va-ca-tion,*" Xander insisted. "The absence of work, the natural state of being, the purpose of life."

"It's boring," Willow said. "But maybe it will pick up this weekend."

"Maybe it will," Buffy agreed, taking a last look around the quiet suburban neighborhood.

Buffy never slept well or deeply anymore, and it didn't take much to jolt her out of bed like a rocket. Still dressed in a clinging sleeveless shirt, she rolled out of bed onto her bare feet and listened to the disturbing sounds coming through her bedroom window. The warm night air brought demented yapping that was unmistakable—the coyotes were on the hunt! They were nearby, coming closer.

She knew instinctively that it was the same pack of coyotes they had met earlier that night. Although it was now close to four o'clock in the morning, they weren't done terrorizing the neighborhood yet. Truthfully, Buffy relished an opportunity to observe the pack without those skeptics, Xander and Willow, slowing her down. She had never seen coyotes that bold, and she wanted to keep an eye on them.

Rising like a wave, the eerie yapping passed over her house like an aural ghost. Buffy pulled on a pair of jeans and her tennis shoes, crawled out the window, and scurried down the roof. By the time she jumped to the ground, all she got was a glimpse of the pack as they charged brazenly down the middle of the street. In the lead was a swift blond canine, clutching something white in its mouth.

In a frenzy of demented yapping, the others

chased it down an alley and were gone a second later. Although she doubted whether she could catch them, Buffy was about to try when she heard a frenzied shout. She turned to see a middle-aged woman in a nightgown bearing down on her.

"Stop them! Stop them!" the woman screamed. "My baby!"

"Your baby!" Buffy said with a gasp. Had they really snatched a baby?

Panting for breath, the distraught woman rushed up to Buffy and grabbed her arm. "They took my Tiger!"

The teenager blinked at her. "Okay, did they take a baby or a tiger? Or was it a baby tiger?"

"Oh, no, my precious *Tiger!*" the woman shrieked. "He's a little pug-nosed chow."

"Oh, a dog," Buffy said, trying not to look relieved. It was terrible that the coyotes had snatched the woman's dog, but that was better than a baby. She remembered similar tragedies in Los Angeles; that's what happened when coyotes went hunting in the suburbs.

"They took him right out of my backyard!" the woman said in a quavering voice. "He was old and infirm, and he couldn't fight back. We have to *save* him!"

Buffy held her hands and tried to be comforting. "I'm sorry, but I don't see how we're going to save Tiger. He was probably dead within seconds of them grabbing him. Besides, there's no way we could catch them."

The distraught woman buried her face in her hands and began to weep, and Buffy glanced around, amazed that nobody else had come out to witness this dramatic scene. Even now, the yelps of the coyotes sounded distant, as if they had only been a passing nightmare.

There wasn't much for Buffy to do but walk her home. "Where do you live?" she asked.

"Can't we do *anything?"* her neighbor blubbered.

"Well, sure, we'll report them to Animal Control, or the dog catcher, or whoever handles stuff like this." Buffy mustered a hopeful smile.

"They won't do anything," the woman grumbled. "Tiger is gone, all thanks to those damn coyotes! It must be Coyote Moon that brought them here. Curse them!"

"Coyote Moon?" Buffy asked warily.

The woman stared grimly down the deserted street, which looked so peaceful that it was hard to imagine it had just been the scene of a grisly hunt and kill. "Coyote Moon comes in August," she intoned, "when it gets hot. It rises red, and it brings the coyotes. That's what my grandmother always said."

"Grandmothers are usually right about that stuff," Buffy remarked lamely, thinking of Grandma Summers playing bridge in Clearwater, Florida.

The woman began to weep uncontrollably, and the Slayer guided her to the sidewalk. "Just point the way home."

She only lived half a block away, yet it took about

ten minutes to walk her home. Buffy listened sympathetically to lighthearted tales about Tiger's exploits. He was a much-beloved little dog, and he had lived a full, spoiled life. Talking seemed to make the woman feel better, and she thanked Buffy profusely.

The teen made sure that her neighbor was safely entrenched behind locked doors before she left her. Although the woman was safe, Tiger was still gone, and nothing would erase the savagery of that attack.

As Buffy walked home, the warm wind again brought the eerie sound of coyotes yipping and yowling. She hoped the pack would move on to some other town or go back to the wilderness, but she wasn't counting on it. Unfortunately, when nasty critters got a taste of Sunnydale, they usually made themselves right at home.

CHAPTER 2

For the next two days, there was no further sign of the coyotes, so Buffy started to relax and fell back into the lazy rhythms of summer. Sleeping in late, waking after her mother had gone to work, eating chocolate brownies for breakfast—it was a life she could get used to.

Buffy had Giles's home telephone number, and she thought about calling him to report the coyotes—but he would probably just scoff at her, too. Thinking about it now, it did seem lame to be afraid of a few wacked-out coyotes, even if they did snack on dog-kabobs. Once school started, Giles would be back in his beloved library, and then she could ask him about coyotes and Coyote Moon. Until then, it was her duty as a teenager to enjoy the long, hot nights.

The coyotes were gone, but signs started popping

up around town advertising the carnival. By the time Friday night rolled around, the Bronze was empty, and every self-respecting teen was eating cotton candy and pitching quarters into fishbowls.

"Cool!" Xander exclaimed as they crested the hill and got their first look at the whirling neon lights of the Ferris wheel, the Octopus ride, the Tilt-a-Whirl, and other stomach-churning delights. Overnight a vacant lot had been turned into a gaudy wonderland, swarming with young people. The tawdry sights and sounds drew them like moths to a patio bug light. Surfer music blasted from crackling speakers, promising the endless summer they were all dreaming about.

Well, all of us but Willow, Buffy thought.

Even from a distance, Buffy could smell the greasy french fries and sugary apples. She heard a jumble of sounds: calliope music from the merry-go-round, screaming girls on the roller coaster, barkers working the crowd, and gasoline generators keeping the lights burning. Buffy knew she should run in the other direction, because all of this was designed to separate her from her hard-earned cash—but her feet began moving of their own will. Transfixed by the throbbing neon lights, Buffy shuffled down the hill toward the carnival.

"Isn't this fun?" Xander asked with a grin.

"Lots of fun," Willow agreed. "I'm just trying to decide whether to have my corn dog first, then throw up—or whether to throw up first, then eat the corn dog. The second way makes more sense, but the corn dog doesn't taste as good."

"That's our Willow, always being practical," Xander said with amusement.

Buffy pulled her eyes reluctantly from the dazzling sights. "Why does it have to be either/or. Why can't you just ignore the rides that make you hurl?"

"They *all* make me hurl," Willow answered. "And I always get talked into going on them anyway."

Xander put his arm around her slender shoulders. "Hey, Willow, to make it easy on you, we'll start with the fun house. We'll work up to the rocket ship thing where you're strapped inside a cage, spinning around. If you're brave enough, maybe *I'll* even buy you a corn dog."

Willow looked plaintively at Buffy. "See what I mean? The only time Xander ever buys me anything is to get me to go on the rides with him." She sighed. "But it works."

"I'm going to be sensible," Buffy vowed. "No upchuck express for me."

"But the roller coaster is calling your name," Xander said with a twinkle in his eye.

"Okay," Buffy admitted. "How did you know I liked roller coasters?"

"Because you're Danger Girl!" he proclaimed.

"That's Vacation Girl," Buffy reminded him.

They walked under banners and lights stuck high on slender wooden poles. Xander pointed toward a weathered metallic skeleton which stood three stories high and was the size of a large barn. The roller coaster didn't look safe to stand under, let alone ride on. As a string of cars rose slowly up the first hill, the tracks clacked ominously, like a busted jackhammer.

"That's a rickety-looking roller coaster," Xander said with a worried grimace. "You know, it's the kind that moans and shakes a lot when you go around the corners."

His theory was verified by the terrified screams that rent the air as the coaster took its first and deepest plunge. Then it whipped noisily around a sharp corner, eliciting more anguished shrieks. Buffy gave Xander a look of dread, which she managed to hold for a few seconds before they both grinned.

"No, I wouldn't like that at all," Buffy said.

"We'll do it first," Xander agreed. "And Willow can hold our food and our stuffed animals."

"No, no," Willow said stalwartly. "It's corn dog express, full speed ahead!"

The three friends were laughing as they entered the giddy realm of the carnival. *It is its own shimmering town,* Buffy thought, *with all the features of a real town.* There was food and drink, none of it even remotely healthy. The music was a jarring combination of surfer records, heavy metal, and gooey kids' songs. There was entertainment, but not even the cleverest boy could win the stupid games, unless he discovered the magic of a first date on a hot summer's night. Then a lucky girl might take home a gigantic stuffed animal.

As they wandered down the midway, Buffy found

herself watching the people more than the attractions. The carnival was packed with teens in muscle shirts and halter tops, hanging all over one another. *Raging hormone time,* Buffy thought. At moments like this, she really regretted being terminally single.

It was bad enough that Willow and Xander knew about her Slayer secret and insisted on helping and/or meddling, as the case may be. A boyfriend would never fit in with her student-by-day, Slayer-by-night lifestyle. As she had discovered, even trying to have a simple date with a guy was way too complicated.

Buffy was afraid to ask Giles what became of Slayers when they got older. She was certain they ended up as old maids and spinsters, or dead. Probably dead.

Still, it would be nice to bump into Angel at a place like this, Buffy thought. She quickly squelched that thought. *Bad Buffy, bad!* Angel was a good vampire, cursed to have a soul and feelings, which made him even weirder than she was. It was better not to think about boys at all, but that was difficult when so many were on display under the sizzling neon.

If the teens from the town looked hot, so did the carnies who ran the rides and games. Buffy was surprised to see that so many of them looked young and buff, not like the grizzled dudes she remembered as a kid. Oh, they were kind of scruffy and dangerous-looking, as if they needed a shave and a new tattoo, but that was part of their charm. So was the leer in their eyes and the promise of fun in their voices.

"A free shot for the woman with the great legs," said a muscular young carny, spinning a basketball on his fingertip. He had a deep tan and about four days' growth of beard; his insouciant smile stopped her cold. Buffy knew that the hoop behind him was a lot smaller than regulation, and a stop to talk to the carny would likely cost her two or three dollars.

"Later," she said, meaning it.

She had to shove Willow out of the way, because she had also stopped to gape at the carny. "Uh, maybe we should play some games," Willow suggested innocently.

"Okay, Miss Money Management—we discussed it," Xander said impatiently. "Ride tickets first, then food, then, if we have any money left over, games."

"For once, he's right," Buffy replied.

"Hello, nurse!" Xander exclaimed as he veered toward a pretty young woman in cut-off shorts and a skimpy top. She smiled like a gypsy as she beckoned him to her booth, which was already crowded with guys. After exchanging worried glances, Buffy and Willow trailed along to see what the scam was all about.

The beautiful dark-haired girl was only the bait. The main attraction was a seedy clown in a dunking machine. With a rainbow wig, streaked makeup, and old clothes, he didn't look like much of a clown; but he was sitting on a wooden plank perched over a big tank of water. The sign said that it cost two dollars to throw five balls at the disc-like target, in the hope of dumping the clown into the water. He looked awfully dry to Buffy.

The clown also had a microphone hanging over his head, and he wasn't afraid to use it. "I've never seen so many beautiful women in one place," he grumbled in a voice that boomed across the midway. "So where did you babes get these *ugly guys?* Man, the dog pound must be empty!"

One clean-cut young man stepped up to the dark-haired girl and declared, "I'll knock him in."

"Two dollars, farm boy," she said in a teasing voice.

"Oh, now we got a local hero!" the clown crowed. "Let's see if you're *man* enough to knock me into the drink. Maybc you can win a kiss from Rose!"

The girl pouted and posed, showing off a rose tattoo on the top of her cleavage, and Xander drooled along with the rest of the guys. Rose collected two dollars from the dazed boy and handed him five old softballs. Buffy and Willow exchanged a sigh. Didn't boys ever learn?

The clown sneered. "What a *wimp!* I bet he can't even *get* it to the target! Go on, wimp, take your best shot!"

Huffing and puffing, the boy wound up and threw. He was wide, but he threw hard and with authority.

"My *grandmother* throws better than that!" the clown roared into his microphone. "But I think the pee-wee league has found a new pitcher!"

In angry succession, the boy hurled four more balls, each one farther away from the target than the one before.

"Come on," Rose said with a purr. "You want to try again?"

"No," the boy muttered, completely embarrassed. "I'm outta here."

Although a lot of people were watching the proceedings, not that many were digging into their pockets for two dollars. The failure of the last contestant had scared some of them away.

"What is this town?" the clown asked. "Sunny Jail?" The kids laughed at the takeoff on the town's name of Sunnydale, and the professional heckler continued. "I don't want to say people are stupid here, but the biggest decision after high school is whether to marry your cousin or your sister."

Laughter and groans came in equal measure, and some of the guys were thinking about parting with their money. Rose turned to Xander and batted her eyelashes. "How about you, big boy? Have *you* got what it takes?"

The teenager turned to mush and nearly melted under the stage, but Rose's dark eyes held him up. When he didn't move fast enough for his wallet, the clown on the platform sneered. "Hey, kid, is that a mustache or a third armpit?"

Buffy had to laugh at that one, and Xander looked at her accusingly. Now there was no hesitation as he reached for his wallet and took out two dollars. He didn't like clowns much, anyway.

"Clown. Water. Prepare to meet," he vowed, and the crowd cheered.

"Money management!" Willow shouted to no avail.

Xander took careful aim at the disc-like target, but it was hardly any bigger than one of the softballs—and it was forty feet away. It would require a perfect throw to soak the obnoxious clown, and Xander would never be confused with a great athlete. His first pitch missed by six feet.

"Omigosh, did he kill anybody?" the clown asked, to much laughter.

"You can do it," Rose said encouragingly.

"Yeah, you can do it!" Willow shouted, not to be outdone.

Xander reached back and threw hard, coming within two feet.

"Visualize it!" Buffy shouted.

"You visualize this," the clown said, staring directly at Buffy. "You and me on a little date, at a fancy French restaurant. We'll order some truffles and some fine wine—I'll get you some soda pop."

She gave him what she hoped was a disgusted look, but his words were having the desired effect on Xander. Looking so angry that he couldn't even see the target, he threw two straight misses. He only had one ball left.

The clown mocked him. "Maybe it would help if we got you a Seeing Eye dog!"

That was it for Buffy. She walked up to Xander and held out her hand. "Time for a relief pitcher."

He looked at her with a mixture of anger and frustration, but relief soon spread across his face. She could see his mind working: *Buffy has perfect coordination, and Buffy could hit that target with any weapon known to mankind. Let Buffy throw the ball.*

"I'm giving her my last ball," Xander said to Rose. He said it apologetically, as if he was sorry that her clown was about to bite it.

"Oh, he's the *supreme* wimp!" the clown hooted. "By all means, give your *girlfriend* the last ball. I'll make it even easier for the little lady. Rose, give her an extra ball from me, too."

"No thanks," Buffy said, hefting the spongy softball. "I'll only need one."

"Awfully confident, aren't you?" Rose sneered.

This was called showing off, Buffy thought, and she shouldn't be doing it. She could imagine the horrified look on Giles's face if he knew what she was up to. *But a Slayer has to do what a Slayer has to do.* At least she was going to make an awful lot of people in the crowd very happy.

The clown was saying something else insulting, but she tuned him out in order to concentrate. Unlike Xander, she *did* visualize the ball leaving her hand on a perfect trajectory and striking the target dead-center. She saw it trip the lever that held up the plank, and she saw the plank drop. She didn't have to visualize the obnoxious clown falling into the water, because she was about to see that for real.

Whirling nonchalantly, Buffy threw the softball on

a line with hardly any arc. It struck the target with a reassuring clang, and the plank dropped with a loud *clack!* She relished the startled look on the clown's face as he plunged into the water with a gushing splash. The crowd went wild, applauding and cheering, and the clown waved from the tank, as if he was taking the bows.

"Nice throw," Rose said, looking suspiciously at Buffy.

"Beginner's luck," the Slayer replied with a cute giggle. She grabbed Xander and tried to pull him away from the carny, but he was still fixated on Rose.

"Hey," Xander said sheepishly, "don't I get a kiss? It was *my* ball, even though she threw it."

Rose leaned over dramatically and whispered to him. "Come back in half an hour, and I'll take my break."

Xander gaped at her, then looked around, as if she had to be speaking to somebody else. Buffy rolled her eyes at how helpless he was around this vamp. That was *vamp* in the old-fashioned sense, because she didn't sense anything undead about the girl. In fact, she seemed to be very lively. Buffy didn't think that Rose was a proper playmate for Xander, although she doubted he would agree.

Ignoring the hound-dog look on his face, Buffy used all her strength to drag Xander away from the exotic carny. Willow cut off his escape route to the rear.

"Money management," Willow insisted.

"Creaky rides! Screaming girls! Whiplash!" Buffy reminded him. "All rides guaranteed to leave your stomach outside your body!"

"Take me wherever you want," Xander said blissfully. He checked his watch. "But you have exactly thirty minutes."

Willow shot a worried look at Buffy, who shrugged helplessly. With the vibes in the air tonight, they would be lucky if it was only Xander who got carried away. Buffy had to admit that Rose was quite an attraction—wild cheerleaders probably couldn't stop Xander from keeping his date.

They rode the roller coaster, and the girls screeched as they roared up and down the rickety peaks. Xander, meanwhile, kept looking at his watch. They rode the Ferris wheel, and Xander worried that they would be stuck at the top for too long. He couldn't even enjoy the fantastic view of the carnival, shimmering like an island of light in the vast dreariness of Sunnydale.

When they got off the Ferris wheel, Buffy noticed a grizzled old carny with oil stains on his face and hands. He stood beside the groaning machinery and slapped a wrench against his palm, watching them walk away. Buffy felt a disturbing sense of déjà vu, as if she had seen him before, looking at her that same way.

At least there went the theory that all the carnies were young and gorgeous. *He* looked like the carnies she remembered from her childhood—gnarly and creepy.

They still had plenty of ride tickets left, but Xander led the way as they drifted back toward the hucksters.

"Free practice shot!" one shouted.

"Everybody's a winner!" another called.

Xander stumbled along, transfixed by the lights, the noise, the games, and the girls. Buffy tried not to be angry with him.

"Hey, Xander, keep it under control. Don't be too eager," she warned. "She said half an hour, not ten minutes."

"Yes, you're better off to keep her waiting," Willow suggested, not sounding very convincing. "And it may only be a fifteen-minute break."

"Fifteen minutes with Rose," Xander said dreamily. "I'll take it."

"I wonder how many guys she's said that to?" Buffy asked.

"Neither one of you is gonna spoil this night," Xander vowed. He checked his watch again, then held it to his ear to make sure it was running, which was dumb, because it was a digital watch.

"Hey, beautiful! Break my heart!" a masculine voice called.

Buffy whirled around to see a tanned blond hunk with sleeves rolled up over brawny muscles. He was the most handsome carny yet, and he was standing in a dart booth, surrounded by posters of hot rods, puppies, TV actors, and bikini babes.

The hunk pointed to a pink heart-shaped balloon on the cork board behind him. "Look how big my heart is. I bet you could break it without half trying."

"Like I'm sure that hasn't happened," she admitted. The heart-shaped balloon was surrounded by smaller balloons and lots of white space. He seemed to be giving away the posters, but she didn't need any more posters in her bedroom. Still, Buffy's feet propelled her toward the booth, and Willow was right beside her.

"Two lovely ladies—it's my lucky night." The carny smiled, revealing hidden dimples in the stubble of his blond beard. A merry twinkle in his blue eyes said he knew his game was a rip-off, but that made it even more fun. He held out three darts to Buffy. "Break it, and anything I have is yours."

Buffy noticed a tattoo on his brawny forearm, but it was so faded that she couldn't tell what it was. She wondered whether the carny was older than he looked.

"Let me try," Willow insisted, cutting in between them. She fixed the carny with her best femme fatale expression, but it was hardly fatal. Nevertheless, the carny was happy to play along, and he flirted brazenly with Willow.

"No rush, little lady, we've got all night. My name is Lonnie."

"Pleased to meet you," she answered cheerfully. "I'm Willow, and this is Buffy." When she glanced back to see what Xander was doing, Buffy finally realized what was going on—Willow was trying to get Xander's attention by flirting with this hunk. Of course, Xander was too busy looking at his watch to care what either one of them was doing.

"What are the rules?" Willow asked.

Reluctantly, Lonnie pulled his eyes away from Buffy to his paying customer. "You give me two dollars, and I give you three really sharp darts. You get three chances to win. Break my heart or break any balloon, and you take your choice of anything I've got."

Willow giggled, and Lonnie motioned around at the posters, most of which were worth about a dollar. "None of them are as pretty as you," he told Willow, who rolled her eyes but giggled in spite of herself.

Not a bad deal, Buffy thought. *Spend two dollars trying to win a prize worth half that.* Most people didn't win, of course, but even if you lost, you still got Lonnie's charming company.

Taking a deep breath as if she were about to run a marathon, Willow hefted the first dart and let it fly. It hit the board, but just barely—near the bottom, far from any balloon. Willow smiled gamely and tried again. This time, her weakly thrown dart hit a balloon and bounced off, without breaking it.

"Hey!" she said in protest. "Are those trick balloons?"

Again Lonnie had to tear his eyes away from Buffy. "They're just regular balloons. Listen, if you miss your last one, I'll give you one more, on the house."

"That's very decent of you," Willow said, sounding pleased. She threw her third dart, and it landed perfectly—in the white space between two balloons.

With a charming smile, Lonnie handed her another dart. "Don't tell my boss," he said.

Willow looked concerned. "Will you get in trouble?"

Lonnie laughed, and it was a warm, decadent sound. "I was *born* in trouble. Go ahead and throw."

Willow took careful aim and threw the last dart; it sailed over the board and stuck in the canvas at the back of the booth.

Lonnie immediately turned his full attention to Buffy. "Your turn to break my heart."

"No thanks," Buffy said, knowing full well she could clean him out of his crummy posters. "I've reached my tacky wall-hangings quota. Maybe later."

"Speaking of later," Lonnie said, leaning intimately toward her, "meet me back here in half an hour, when I take my break."

"Give *me* a break." Buffy groaned. "Are all of you trained with the same come-on line?"

"Huh?" Lonnie asked.

Willow broke in with nervous laughter. "Don't listen to her, Lonnie. What were you saying about taking a break?"

But he wasn't through with Buffy yet. "Are you shutting me down?" he asked incredulously.

"Guess it doesn't happen too often," Buffy replied, getting ticked. "About as often as somebody wins a prize around here."

"Hey, it's your loss," Lonnie said. His blue eyes weren't so merry anymore.

Buffy started to drag her friend away from the booth, but Lonnie produced three more darts. "Not so fast. I like you, Willow. I want to give you another chance. Have a free play!"

Willow's eyes widened with excitement, and she yanked her arm away from Buffy. Never taking her eyes off the handsome carny, she said, "Buffy, you should be nice to Lonnie—he's giving me a free play."

"Yeah," Buffy muttered. "Why don't you stick around for his break? I hear it'll be in half an hour."

Buffy turned to look for Xander, but all she saw was the back of his shirt disappearing into the crowd. He was headed in the direction of the dunking machine, and Buffy didn't think she could catch him. Probably a master vampire couldn't stop him.

Willow smiled coyly as she took the darts from Lonnie. The handsome carny shot a glance at Buffy, then put his arm around the slender girl's shoulders. "Let me show you a technique that never fails."

Buffy groaned and started to stalk away, disgusted with her friends. After a few angry strides, she realized that she was really disgusted with herself. Why should Willow and Xander be deprived of a little fun, just because *she* felt deprived? It wasn't their fault that she was a Slayer and couldn't have a normal boyfriend. It wasn't their fault that on a night ripe with romance, she was all alone. Even around a bunch of people, Buffy always felt alone.

In every generation, there is a Slayer. Not a bunch of them, just *one.* She was the freak—even the people who worked this seedy carnival were normal compared to her.

Buffy stepped out of the circle of neon light and found herself on the outskirts of the carnival. She could still hear the blaring music and smell the greasy food, but she wasn't part of it anymore. From outside, she could see the weather-beaten trailers, dirty tents, snaking wires, and chugging generators that kept the fake city alive.

With her senses finally cleared, she had time to think. There *was* something wiggins about most of the carnies being young and gorgeous. She would deny ever thinking it, but gorgeous people hitting on Xander and Willow was also off the wall. Maybe she was just being paranoid, but it was never far from Buffy's mind that this unlikely town was located on the Hellmouth. Nasty types were just naturally drawn here.

While she had a few minutes by herself, Buffy decided to look around. It was dark behind the trailers and tents, but she didn't need much light to see.

She wasn't looking for anything in particular—just looking. Ever since Buffy was a little girl, she had been the type of person who peeked inside people's medicine chests when she visited their bathrooms. She was naturally curious, and maybe that was all part of who—and what—she was. For a Slayer, it was either be nosy or be dead.

Ripe smells of rotting fruit and putrid meat twisted her head around, and she saw a row of garbage cans in the shadows behind the fun house. Looking through people's trash was not something Buffy enjoyed doing, but it was the next best thing when there wasn't a medicine chest handy. Breathing through her mouth, she walked gingerly toward the dump.

The trash cans were filled to overflowing, and there was garbage all over the ground as well. Since the carnival had just opened that night, most of this stuff had to belong to the carnival workers themselves, Buffy thought. With the toe of her boot, she kicked through old food wrappers, eggshells, greasy paper towels, rotten fruit, and the usual refuse of society.

The carnies' garbage was disgusting but nothing special, and she was about to explore elsewhere when something shiny caught her eye. Buffy kicked a gooey rag off the object and bent down to see a curled strap of red leather with shiny silver studs and a silver buckle. She turned it over and saw metal tags hanging from it.

It's a dog collar.

With a feeling of dread expanding in her stomach like a wad of cotton candy, Buffy picked up the dog collar and read the tags. One tag was a dog license, and the other had a name inscribed on it. The name was Tiger.

Licking her dry lips, Buffy remembered a few nights back, when the pack of coyotes had snatched a dog named Tiger off her street. How come the poor dog's collar had ended up here?

A twig snapped, and Buffy jumped to her feet and whirled around. The grizzled old carny from the Ferris wheel now stood about ten feet away from her, staring at her with pale, rheumy eyes. Again she was sure that she had seen those eyes before somewhere. More troubling was the fact that he had sneaked awfully close to her before she heard him, which wasn't typical. She also didn't like the way he was slapping his heavy wrench against his grimy palm.

"What are you looking for?" he demanded.

Buffy held Tiger's collar behind her back and stuffed it into her belt. His eyes were so familiar. But from where? Buffy gasped as she finally remembered where she had seen the man's eyes before.

But that is impossible!

"Who are you?" he snarled. His pale eyes flashed with anger, and he lifted the wrench as he strode toward her.

Chapter 3

Buffy leaped away from the creepy carny, but she didn't assume her fighting stance. She still wanted to look helpless, if possible. She checked out escape routes from the rear of the carnival, and she saw cars parked nearby.

"Listen," she said. "I didn't mean to cause trouble. Actually, I . . . I was feeling a little gross from all the rides, and I was looking for a good place to heave. Is this okay? Can I heave right here?"

The old carny stopped in his tracks. Even the baddest dude didn't want somebody to hurl all over him. Buffy stared at the man, certain that she had to be mistaken about him. Could he really be the old coyote she had seen on the street a few nights ago? He was staring at her just as that coyote had stared at her, and his eyes were eerily similar.

But that meant he was a *werecoyote,* if there was

such a thing. Well, Buffy decided, if there were werecoyotes, sooner or later they would end up in Sunnydale.

He took another step toward her, and she began to gag and bent over. "Look out!" she warned.

The old carny quickly backed away. "This is not a good place for you to be. Try the Porta Potties at the end of the midway."

"Porta Potties," she said gratefully. "What a good idea." She staggered back toward the gaudy lights and manic music. "Thanks a lot, Mister . . . uh—"

"Hopscotch. The name is Hopscotch."

"I'll remember that," she said truthfully. If she was right about Hopscotch—that he could turn himself into a coyote—then maybe some of the other carnies were also in the pack. Come to think of it, the carnies acted like a pack, working together to run the rides, games, and food stands. She had to find Xander and Willow before they got too hung up on Rose and Lonnie!

Buffy ran first to the dunking machine, but there was now a pretty redheaded girl collecting money and handing out softballs. Rose was gone, and Xander was nowhere in sight—so they were probably together, taking the fabled break. The last thing Buffy wanted to do was attract even more attention by asking a lot of questions, so she dashed off to Lonnie's dart booth.

The blond hunk was also missing, and so was Willow. Feeling worried and slightly jealous, Buffy wandered down the midway, looking for her friends.

They had been such fools—they hadn't even arranged for a place to meet in case they got split up. And, boy, had they gotten split up.

After a few minutes of roaming through the swirling lights, pounding music, and laughing teens, Buffy began to relax. Once again, the carnival seemed like nothing but harmless fun on a hot summer's night. How could she think those cute carnies were werecoyotes? It was a ridiculous leap of faith, even for Buffy.

For the moment, she decided, she would keep quiet about her suspicions. More than likely, Xander and Willow would be disappointed by their exotic dates, and life would get back to what passed for normal.

Buffy spotted Cordelia and a few other acquaintances from school. They didn't have dates, either, which made her feel better, and she briefly crashed their group. Cordelia was her usual snotty self, but it felt good not to be alone. Buffy kept her eyes open for Xander and Willow.

She finally spotted them both, walking happily together and acting as if *they* were on a date. *If only Xander would wake up and smell the garlic,* Buffy thought. He couldn't do any better than Willow, who idolized him. Buffy fantasized that they had been stood up by Rose and Lonnie and had discovered each other on this romantic night.

She slipped away from Cordelia and her friends and headed them off. "Hey, guys, what's happening?"

Xander grinned as if he was the coyote who ate the dog. "We had a great time."

"You two?" Buffy asked hopefully.

"Yeah," Xander answered with a worldly chuckle. "Me and Rose. I got my *kiss.*"

"I had a great time with Lonnie, too," Willow insisted. "But he had to go back to work."

"How tragic," Buffy said sarcastically.

"But we're going to double-date tomorrow," Willow said.

"You *what!*" Buffy exclaimed. "The *four* of you?"

"It's just a lunch date," Willow replied, "before the carnival opens. They're going to give us a behind-the-scenes tour."

"Maybe you could tag along, like a fifth wheel." Xander glanced at Willow. "We wouldn't mind, would we?"

"Not at all," she answered cheerfully.

"Thanks, but I have to trim my toenails," Buffy muttered. "Willow, could I talk to you for a second?"

"Sure." She smiled innocently at Xander, then allowed Buffy to drag her behind a lemonade stand.

"I know that Xander has no sense when it comes to women," the Slayer whispered, "but what's *your* excuse?"

"Lonnie was a perfect gentleman," Willow answered, sounding surprised and a little disappointed. "If I can double-date with Rose and Xander, I can keep my eye on Xander."

"Okay, that makes sense," Buffy said with relief.

"But these aren't choirboys running this place. I want you to be real careful."

Willow frowned and put her hands on her narrow hips. "It's only a date, Buffy. Do I tell *you* to be careful when you go out on a date?"

"You could," Buffy said, "*if* I ever went out on a date."

"But when you hang out with Angel, he's a lot more dangerous than these people."

"That's debatable." Buffy took a few deep breaths, knowing that her suspicions would sound crazy to Willow and Xander, even though they had seen a lot of crazy things since meeting her. She had to have more proof than a dog collar in the trash.

Xander poked his head around the corner of the stand, and he was smirking. "Are you ladies discussing *me?* I'm very popular with the ladies tonight."

Buffy rolled her eyes and bit her tongue. "Xander, I just want you to be way on guard around these people, that's all."

"Ah, jealousy—it's not pretty, even on you, Buffy," he said smugly.

"No, just a use of brain cells." Buffy sighed, knowing it was pointless to reason with Xander about women. "Listen, your new friends went back to work, so now we can go back to the original agenda—having fun. Are you ready to ride some more rides and eat some food with no nutritional value? I'm getting hungry!"

Xander looked sheepishly at the ground. "I, um . . . I spent the rest of my money on games."

"Me, too," Willow admitted.

Buffy tried not to laugh in their faces. "Okay, my treat. But if any more carnies make goo-goo eyes at you, you just keep on walking."

"I'm content with Rose," Xander said blissfully.

"This is so touching, I'm gonna hurl," Buffy muttered. "Come on, I smell corn dogs."

They went to the front of the lemonade stand and were reading the menu, when Buffy felt eyes on the back of her neck. She turned to see the old carny, Hopscotch, standing across the midway, watching her. She had a feeling he would be watching her for the rest of the night, and whenever she returned to the carnival.

Well, Buffy decided, the next time he and his friends ventured into the streets of Sunnydale, she would be watching *them.*

Much later that Friday night, when Buffy heard the coyotes howl, she was ready. She rolled out of bed fully dressed, wearing binoculars around her neck and her best running shoes. She bounded out the window while the cries of the pack were still fresh on the wind.

I knew *they would be going out tonight,* she thought with satisfaction.

After leaping to the ground, Buffy hid behind a tree in her yard. The night sky was full of clouds, but a translucent glow high in the heavens revealed the hiding place of a bright moon. With all the moonlight, she had no problem finding the pack of scruffy canines romping down the street, sniffing about. They didn't seem to be on the scent of any prey—yet.

Although they acted as if they owned the streets, word of their last visit must have gotten out. Buffy heard muffled barking, but it sounded as if all the neighborhood dogs were safely ensconced behind locked doors.

As the coyotes loped farther down the street, Buffy lifted the binoculars to watch them from a distance—she didn't want to get any closer than necessary. The suburban street looked deserted, except for her, the coyotes, and ghostly wisps of fog.

The mist was thickest in the low-lying dips in the road, where it was almost impossible to see the coyotes. She hoped the fog wouldn't get any worse, or her binoculars would be useless.

Buffy didn't move from her hiding place until the coyotes loping in the rear were almost out of sight. She dashed down the street, moving from tree to tree and house to house for cover. This was an older suburb with lots of big oaks and sycamores, and she was able to keep hidden. She knew that the wind might carry her scent and alert the coyotes to her presence, but she had no control over that. Luckily, they were running against the wind, looking for the scent of prey, and she was downwind of them.

For several blocks, she kept the coyotes in view with her binoculars, until one of them gave an excited howl and dashed off. The others gave chase like greyhounds at a dog race, and their yipping was frenzied and excited. *They must have found something to hunt!* Buffy put her head down and ran as fast as she could to catch up with them.

As she cautiously rounded the corner of a house, the Slayer saw the pack of coyotes at the end of the block, huddled under a tree. Some of them ran frantically in circles, while others sprang up and down. Most of them sat and stared forlornly into the high branches.

Beyond the coyotes was a black, open space with spooky tendrils of fog drifting through marble tombstones. A chill wind blew from the old cemetery and made Buffy shiver. Since coming to Sunnydale, she had often encountered vampires in the crumbling mausoleums of this place. In fact, it was practically a vampire retirement home.

Staying in the shadows so as not to be seen, Buffy lifted her binoculars to her eyes. She tried to forget her memories of the cemetery in order to concentrate on her mission. *What do the coyotes find so interesting in that tree?*

By watching their eyes and where they were jumping, she pinpointed something large and tawny-colored, trying to crawl to the uppermost branches. One of those thin branches snapped, and the poor thing plummeted toward the slavering jaws below. The coyotes went nuts, yapping and leaping in a frenzy, but their prey managed to get a grasp at the last second and swing itself to safety. It gave a pitiful yowl for help.

The coyotes had treed a cat! Not content with dog-kabobs, they were going after kitty-kabobs!

Buffy knew she couldn't stand idly by and let them munch on a kitty after playing football with it for a while. She had to intervene, but then she would lose her opportunity to observe them unseen. At the moment, they were acting disgustingly like regular coyotes—as if nothing could be more exciting than treeing a cat. If she were logical, she would forget all about her crazy theory and go home to bed. After all, coyotes had to eat, too.

Fortunately, Buffy had never given in to logic. She had to save the kitty, but how? In a melee, she wasn't sure she could fight the whole pack of coyotes at once. Three or four she could handle, but not fifteen or twenty. But if she waited too long trying to think of a plan, the kitty might be toast.

Suddenly, the scene brightened as if somebody had turned on a giant street lamp. Buffy looked up to see the clouds parting overhead, and an almost-full moon gleamed in the heavens like a beacon. The yipping of the coyotes stopped, and they all looked at once at the moon, ignoring the cat. They held so still, it was as if the moon were a glow-in-the-dark satellite dish and they were receiving signals.

Buffy hugged the side of the house, hoping not to be spotted by their sharp eyes. She needn't have worried, because the pack turned in unison and bolted in the opposite direction—toward the cemetery. With high leaps, they cleared the wrought-iron fence and vanished amidst the lonely tombstones and tendrils of fog.

There seemed little point in staying hidden—unless the pack stopped, she would never catch them. Buffy jogged down the sidewalk directly under the tree where the frightened cat had taken refuge. She looked up and saw the feline clinging to a branch like a stone gargoyle.

"You're down to eight lives now," she whispered. "Go on home."

At once, the cat leaped to the ground and scurried across the street and under a house. Buffy nodded with relief and continued her run toward the cemetery. With an effortless leap, she cleared the spear tips of the iron fence and landed on the soft earth of a large grave. She rolled onto the grass, jumped to her feet, and brushed herself off.

It was an old cemetery, and they packed them in, except for the mausoleums and monuments in the well-to-do section toward the middle. Despite the bright moon, it seemed darker here. The cemetery was in a vast hollow, so the fog was thicker; and there were no street lamps or house lights to spoil the darkness.

Buffy put the binoculars to her eyes, not expecting to find the coyotes unless by some miracle they stopped. If they were using the cemetery only as a shortcut to get somewhere else, she had probably already lost them.

Patiently she scanned the landscape of gnarly trees and creepy tombstones for any trace of movement.

Buffy also listened for their cries, but she could hear nothing except the wind rustling ominously through the trees. Somewhere a gate clacked open and shut in the wind, lending an eerie rhythm to the sounds of the cemetery.

I should've brought some backup. A nice stake or two . . . just in case. Squelching her fear, Buffy kept the binoculars glued to her eyes. She finally spotted a four-legged figure cutting through a patch of fog. It raced across the ground, then leaped to the top of a mausoleum. Fog obscured her vision, but at least she had a direction in which to head. Of course, the animal was headed toward the well-to-do section with all the fancy mausoleums and monuments.

Going back into stealth mode, Buffy padded quietly from one tombstone to another, using the fog for cover. She kept her eyes open for other denizens of the cemetery, but they seemed to be minding their own business. Like the rest of the town, they wanted nothing to do with this weird pack of coyotes. Buffy was the only one foolish enough to chase them around in the dead of night—through a cemetery.

She saw several more fleeting figures, and they seemed to be gathering around a tall white tombstone. It looked like the spire of the Washington Monument, only it had a marble ball on the top. When Buffy looked through the binoculars, she saw that the ball was actually the moon, complete with craters.

Thanks to a hill and a copse of trees between her and the grave, Buffy couldn't see more than two or three coyotes at a time. They seemed to be running around in circles, yet they weren't barking and yipping as if they had cornered some unfortunate prey.

Buffy knew she had to sneak closer to see what they were doing. Her usual style was to walk right into danger, make a few clever quips to loosen everyone up, then kick butt. She wasn't used to creeping about on her delicate knees, but this was intelligence gathering. It had to be done. Coyotes were known for being unpredictable and weird, so before she could go to Giles with her suspicions about *these* coyotes, she had better be sure.

The Slayer scrambled forward through the tall, damp grass, resting behind tombstones and tree trunks. She kept moving until she reached the top of the hill, where she finally had a decent view of the crazed coyotes. Buffy got down on her belly between two tree trunks and crawled to the edge of the mossy hill.

She was no expert on coyotes, but this bunch seemed to be acting strangely. They were running in a counterclockwise circle around the spire and the old grave, which was covered with withered flowers. But that wasn't the strangest thing they were doing.

Every few seconds, one of the coyotes would leap out of the frenzied race and attack the grave. Whimpering pathetically, the coyote would dig a shallow hole, tossing the withered flowers in every direction. Just as suddenly, the coyote would stop digging and rejoin the race, and another one would take its place.

If the whole pack really started digging, they could unearth the coffin in a few minutes, Buffy thought. It didn't seem as if they were really trying to dig up the grave—they were only *pretending*. But why? She watched this strange ceremony, getting more puzzled by the second. *What in blazing underpants are they doing?*

Pretend or not, coyotes digging up a grave was still enough to give her a major case of the willies. Buffy made a mental note to come back in the daytime and see who was buried under the moon spire. It must have been somebody who was important or rich, because that massive headstone didn't come cheap.

Mixed in with the panting and running sounds, Buffy heard a low growl. It sounded way too close and too loud—in fact, it almost whispered in her ear. She heard long jaws clack together, and she knew a beast was right behind her, ready to attack. Buffy whirled around and lifted her hand to ward off the attack, but it didn't come—at least not at that instant.

Through the mist she saw the old coyote with the yellow eyes, standing about ten feet away. It drew back its slobbering lips, showing her rows of jagged teeth. The hair on their necks stood like bad punk haircuts.

Hopscotch! Buffy thought grimly. If she wasn't sure before, she was sure now. She started inching away, wondering how far she could run before the scruffy coyote could pounce on her back or sink its teeth into her leg.

The wise old hunter was too crafty to take her on all by itself. It lifted its snout and howled in a chilling tone that sounded like Mom calling the kids to dinner. When it was answered by excited yipping, Buffy bounded to her feet and looked for an escape route.

There was none. In every direction, all she saw were wild-eyed, snarling coyotes charging toward her!

CHAPTER 4

As the coyotes vaulted toward her, howling like the possessed, Buffy crouched in the graveyard. She saw a shadow move on her right, and she spun her left foot just in time to catch Hopscotch before it could reach her throat. She kicked the old coyote a dozen feet into the bushes, then she leaped skyward as two more coyotes crashed under her feet.

Landing on top of the dazed beasts, the Slayer pounded their jaws shut with flying fists. She looked around—still more were coming from every direction. They were all slashing teeth and smelly hair!

Buffy did a cartwheel, kicking two of the coyotes in their toothy chops, and she twirled like a hula hoop down the hill—straight into the mysterious grave. She crashed in a heap on top of the wilted flowers, and the coyotes howled with indignation. Their anguished cries brought her quickly back to her senses, and she staggered to her feet. With no other options and coyotes bearing down on her, Buffy started to run.

Two feet weren't as good as four, and the pack of predators was closing in fast, snapping at her heels and calves. In desperation, Buffy leaped ten feet into the air and landed on top of one of the old mausoleums. She weaved back and forth, trying to get her footing on the slippery marble roof—it was raked at an angle like the roof on a real house.

Coyotes could jump, too, and several of them came hurtling toward her. Buffy lashed out with her fists at the beasts, but they were wiry and quick—and hard to hit. She didn't dare use her feet, because she didn't want to lose her balance and tumble off her perch. Since she couldn't land a full punch, she hit the coyotes just hard enough to knock them off course and send them spiraling to the ground.

When they started leaping at her from all four sides at once, Buffy was forced to whirl around and kick with her feet. Twice she nearly fell into their deadly jaws, but she caught her balance at the last moment. The excitement of the hunt drove them into a frenzy, and they yipped and yapped as if Buffy were a cat caught in a tree.

From a distance, it's entertaining to watch this behavior; but when you're the prey, it's no fun at all!

With her lightning reflexes, Buffy was able to defend the roof of the mausoleum, but she never got a moment's rest from the enraged canines. Buffy quickly realized that a persistent attack would wear her down. There were enough attackers that some could take breathers, while she had to fight desperately every second. Her coordination and strength couldn't hold out forever!

From her precarious perch, Buffy spotted another mausoleum two hundred feet away; she knew it well, and hated it. Inside that dreaded mausoleum was a secret passageway which led underground to a vampire lair. *Who knows what's waiting there?*

With her feet slipping off the cold marble and her arms getting heavy from smashing at teeth and snouts, Buffy knew she had to do something fast. She dropped into a crouch, sprang forward, and leaped as far as she could off the roof of the mausoleum.

She cleared the first ring of coyotes and landed next to one that was taking a rest. Instinctively, she grabbed the surprised canine by its bushy tail, swung him around, and threw him into the others. That slowed their pursuit by a second or two, which was all she wanted.

Running all out, Buffy tore through the cemetery with a pack of Cujos nipping at her heels. She could see her goal, the old mausoleum, shimmering in the fog. But would she make it?

Sensing that she might escape, the coyotes made frantic leaps and landed on her back. Buffy stumbled and nearly went down under their wiry limbs and sharp claws, but she tossed them off like an ugly coat and ducked inside the tomb.

Fighting back half a dozen snarling coyotes, Buffy leaned against the heavy marble door. Only the

Slayer's extraordinary strength saved her as she succeeded in slamming the door shut.

Gasping for breath, she slumped against the cold marble and gazed at her gloomy surroundings. An old crypt, peeling walls, mountains of dust and debris—it looked just like her room. For all her cleverness, she had locked herself in a place that was practically a vampire's rec room.

However, Buffy wasn't about to go outside. Deprived of their sport, the coyotes yapped and yowled in protest, and she could still feel them pressing against the door. There was only one way out, and she had to go *down* before she could go *up*.

Buffy moved reluctantly away from the door, afraid they would discover that she wasn't holding it shut. Overcoming her fear, she ran toward the secret passageway and ducked inside. There came a crash as the marble door collapsed to the floor, and coyotes poured through a cloud of ancient dust.

In the dim light, she saw the lead coyotes skid to a stop and back off, whimpering. They sensed something wrong with this place, and she couldn't blame them. Nevertheless, others behind them were trying to push their way in—the thrill of the hunt was more powerful than a few pangs of fear!

Buffy couldn't see any point in standing around watching, because every second counted. She dropped into a crouch and scurried down the dank tunnel, trying not to brush against the slimy, smelly mold that coated the walls. If she met a vampire down here, she had no ammo—not so much as a toothpick! If a vampire met her tonight, it was his good luck, because she was through fighting for one night.

Occasionally, Buffy stopped to listen and glance down the tunnel behind her. As far as she could tell, the coyotes were not pursuing her. Nevertheless, she didn't want to hang around to see if they changed their minds—she just kept plowing ahead.

Her superb vision and unfailing sense of direction led her to a metal utility ladder, and she began to climb. After pushing off a heavy manhole cover, Buffy emerged in the middle of a power plant, surrounded by electrical wires and towering transformers. *That's all right—they're better than the coyotes.*

She looked down at her clothes and saw that her jacket, jeans, and T-shirt were ripped and stained, but somehow the binoculars still hung around her neck. Amazingly enough, she had been saved by the vampires' tunnels. The undead had wisely kept out of the way tonight, and the coyotes had recognized their stench in the mausoleum. She had to think about all of this—and tell Giles.

Nursing sore muscles and numerous scratches and bruises, Buffy climbed slowly over the fence and shuffled home through the deserted streets.

The Slayer jumped out of bed and stared bleary-eyed at her alarm clock. After she realized that it was after ten o'clock, she cursed herself for sleeping in. Of course, she had stayed up late last night and had spent the wee hours of the morning dodging a pack of coyotes through a vampire playground, but that was no excuse.

Wearily, she recalled that it was Saturday, and the first thing she had to do was see Giles. She grabbed her clothes.

Stumbling downstairs to the kitchen, Buffy found a note from her mom saying she was off playing golf. *Golf? They must put something in the water of this place that warps people's minds,* Buffy thought. *Mom has never played golf in Los Angeles—that is Dad's job.*

Well, her mom's absence was a blessing, because Buffy didn't care to explain why the clothes she was stuffing into a garbage bag were all ripped up. The only person she wanted to talk to was Giles.

When she called the librarian's private number, he didn't answer. *Where could he be?* she thought angrily. *Giles doesn't have a life.* She thought about how school was starting in a week or so, and she wondered if the high school could be open for staff preparation and student enrollment. It was worth a try. Even if the school was closed, she could sneak into the library and try to find books about coyotes . . . and werecoyotes. *Didn't Willow say she'd done a report on coyotes?* Then the library was the place to start.

When Buffy got to school, she was relieved to see several cars in the parking lot. For sure, they weren't students showing up early. Walking quickly past the windows so as not to be seen, Buffy slipped in a side door and dashed to the library. As soon as she pushed open the unlocked door, she knew the Watcher was in attendance. The place had a musty smell that was like Giles's personal cologne.

She found him behind his stacks, bent over a pile of magazines. "Hello, Buffy," he said cheerfully. "What brings you to school before absolutely necessary? Not studying, I'm sure."

"Believe it or not, that sounds better than the real reason," the Slayer said glumly, "but I'm here on official business."

The handsome Englishman gazed over the top of his glasses. "Do you mean the undead?"

"No, I mean the unbathed and untrimmed. I'm talking about coyotes."

Giles smiled and picked up a catalog of computer furniture. "Coyotes are very common in this area. I've enjoyed hearing their cries the last few nights."

"Well, I haven't," Buffy snapped, "because I've been out there on the street, part of their dog fest." She held out a forearm that had a nice grid of scratch marks on it.

"Oh, my!" Giles said with concern. "Have you had these wounds treated?"

"Later. I expect to get a lot more of them before I'm done."

"Why fight coyotes?" Giles asked in astonishment. "They're usually not a danger to humans."

Buffy rolled her eyes and began to pace. "Before I

go into the gory details, is it possible for there to be *werecoyotes?"*

"Certainly," Giles answered. "The phenomenon of humans turning into animals has been reported in the folklore of every culture on earth. In Africa, there are werecrocodiles; in the South Pacific, were-sharks. Werewolves are simply the best known in this country because of our European influence. I believe there are tales of werecoyotes in Native American folklore."

"Can you look it up?" Buffy asked worriedly.

Giles moved stiffly up the stairs and into the stacks of rare books that were kept at the back of the library. He seldom allowed anyone to go into the "Reference Only" section unless he accompanied them. With a troubled frown, Buffy slowly followed him.

Hesitantly, Giles asked, "What makes you think these coyotes you battled were, in reality, human?"

"The way they *looked* at me. Bad breath. Lazy attitude. And a pierced nose," Buffy answered. "And the wiggin' out they were doing in the cemetery. That's our next stop."

"It is?" Giles asked warily. He stopped at a shelf of old books at the back of the room, perused the titles, and pulled out four dusty volumes.

"Why would someone want to be a coyote?" Buffy asked.

Giles frowned thoughtfully. "In this modern age, it would be foolish to be a werewolf. Wolves are too rare, except in the wilderness of places like Alaska and Siberia. But if you were a coyote, you could roam all of the western United States, much of Mexico and Canada, and live close to people. No one would think it odd to see you on the street. After all, coyotes usually don't attack humans."

"Well, these do," Buffy muttered.

Giles opened a book, flipped a few pages, and pointed to a passage. "'Coyote is a popular character in Native American literature and mythology. He's the hero of many tales, and he's usually depicted as a trickster. He's a cunning, curious figure with a penchant for the ladies. Coyote has been known to exchange his skin with that of a man in order to bed the man's wife.'"

The proper librarian raised an eyebrow at this improper suggestion, then went on, "'In one story, Coyote was given the job of guarding the moon, but he used his lofty position to spy on humans and learn their secrets. Coyote is often associated with the moon.'"

"No kidding," Buffy muttered. "*Were*coyotes we're talking about, not *storybook* coyotes."

Giles leveled her with a gaze. "You do know that coyotes are famous for their odd ways. I don't know what you saw them doing, but it could be a natural behavior."

"Giles, remember your job description," Buffy said with frustration. "I decide what's wiggins, and you decide what it is."

"Uh, yes, I see," the librarian said, adjusting his glasses and gazing deeper into his tome. Buffy hated putting the Watcher in his place, but Giles had to trust her gut instinct on this.

"You can laugh at me later, if I'm wrong," she promised.

"I've learned not to laugh at you," Giles said testily. He flipped a few more pages.

After a few minutes of reading, he reported, "I can't find anything about werecoyotes in particular, but there's plenty in here about skinwalkers. You might recall, a skinwalker is a type of sorcerer in Native American tradition. A skinwalker can turn himself into an animal by wearing its skin and performing a secret ceremony. Skinwalkers often live in groups away from other people, and they are considered dangerous and to be avoided."

Buffy shuddered. "That sounds like them, all right. Then I should look for coyote skins."

"I believe that shooting and skinning coyotes is illegal," Giles replied. "Are you ever going to tell me what happened to you?"

"Yes, while you drive me over to the cemetery. First, one more question. Do you know what a Coyote Moon is?"

"I presume it's a phase of the moon and not some new restaurant."

"Moon phase, not burrito phase."

Giles set down his stack of Native American books and searched out a new volume. After a moment of study, he said, "Yes, it's here—a rare phase of the moon. I'm sure you know what a Blue Moon is."

Buffy nodded confidently. "Sure, a song they play on the oldies channel."

The librarian winced. "No, it's the second full moon of the month. Of course, most months don't have two full moons, so a Blue Moon is relatively unusual."

He located a passage in his book and began to read: "'*Coyote Moon* is a folk term used in the southwestern United States for a rare phase of the moon. A Coyote Moon is a Blue Moon which rises red on the ninth lunar month in August. The appearance of a Coyote Moon is often associated with trickery and magic.'"

"And all that other wiggins stuff about coyotes," Buffy added.

Giles squinted thoughtfully. "This is late August—the right time of year for a Coyote Moon. I haven't gotten out much, but I think it's nearly a full moon."

"It is, believe me."

"I should run some calculations and see if a Coyote Moon is coming tonight or tomorrow."

"Later," Buffy replied. "That was just something I heard—it might not be related. Right now, we've got to go to the cemetery and see whose grave was getting the coyote treatment. Then warn Willow and Xander."

Giles snapped his book shut. "You don't have any proof at all about these so-called werecoyotes, do you?"

"Nope," she admitted. "If I saw one of them pull

on a ratty old coyote skin and morph into a wild animal, I would tell you."

"All right," Giles said, tapping the pockets of his sweater-vest. "Let me find my car keys and get a notebook, and we'll be on our way."

Willow studied Lonnie's chiseled features, blond stubble of beard, and blue eyes, and she thought: *It's probably hard to take a bath when you're living in a vacant lot.* Perhaps that explained the earthy odor emanating from his person. A lot of girls wouldn't mind it—and Willow wasn't exactly gagging—but she did like her dates to be a bit more well groomed than Lonnie.

She liked them like Xander. Well, normally she liked Xander's style, but he had also affected the scruffy carnival look—greasy jeans, a stained T-shirt, and that mustache thing under his lip. *The third armpit,* she thought with a chuckle. Lonnie, Xander, and Rose turned to look at her.

"Something funny?" Rose asked with a sneer.

"No," Willow answered, stirring her soda with her straw. "I'm just having fun."

"Good," Lonnie said with an easy smile.

The four of them were sitting outside at a table and chairs by a corn dog and lemonade stand. Because the carnival wasn't open yet and the rides weren't running, the only people milling around were the carnies and their invited guests. Several kids from town had apparently struck up friendships with the carnies—Willow saw about half a dozen of them.

It would be great to hang out with Lonnie and Xander at the closed carnival, Willow thought, *if only I can get rid of Rose.* For some reason, the sexy dark-haired girl didn't seem to like Willow very much. Or maybe she was just a naturally obnoxious person, like Cordelia.

"Where's your other friend?" Rose asked.

"My other friend?" Willow smiled. "Oh, you mean Buffy. I almost expected her to be here."

"And crash our date?" Xander muttered. "I hope not. Buffy doesn't date very much."

"Why?" Lonnie asked.

Willow shot Xander a warning look, and he shrugged. "She's sort of like . . . like a nun."

"She didn't dress like a nun," Lonnie said with a grin.

"She's a junior nun," Xander answered.

Rose shook her head. "Nun or no nun, that was a great throw she made last night, the one that sank Eddie. She should be pitching in the big leagues."

"She's more the cheerleader type," Willow remarked.

"Why are we talking about *her?*" Xander asked, grabbing Rose's hand and gazing into her dark, vivid eyes. "There's only one girl in the whole world for me—my Rose of San Antonio."

Now Willow began to gag, but she kept her cool. "What are we going to do next?" she asked brightly.

"Let me see," Lonnie said, tapping his chiseled chin. "We showed you the office, the light panel, the motors, the trailers, the generators, and the trucks. And the air compressor."

"I'll never forget the air compressor," Willow said, trying to sound enthusiastic.

"Would you like to see where we sleep?" Rose asked.

Xander nodded as if his head was on a spring, but he tried to stay cool. "Yeah, yeah! That would be great!"

"Where you sleep?" Willow repeated uncertainly. "Don't you sleep . . . right here?"

Lonnie gave her a dimpled smile. "Well, not right here in the dirt. We each have our own trailer, although some of us have roommates. Rose and I have seniority, so we don't have roommates. Do we, Rose?"

"Not unless we want them," she said with a sly smile. The carny jumped up from the table and pulled Xander up with her. "Enough talk, let's party."

Xander grinned stupidly, as if he had been hit on the head by a baseball bat. Like a farmer leading a lamb to the slaughter, Rose dragged the poor boy away from the table. "See you later!" she called back.

Willow leaped up. "Wait a minute! Aren't we going with them?"

"Why?" Lonnie asked, rising to his feet and towering over her. He touched her cheek with his callused hand and angled her face toward his. "There's only so much you can do on a double date, before you have to make it a single date."

Reluctantly, Willow pulled away from him. "But I . . . I haven't seen the *fun house* yet! Yes, I always dreamed of being inside a fun house . . . when there was nobody else there."

She turned and looked for Xander and Rose, but they were gone. In a panic, she feared that Xander might be gone forever. How could she, or even Buffy, compete with a girl who had tattoos?

"Okay," Lonnie said. "Let's make your dreams come true."

Wrapping his brawny arm around her slender waist, he led Willow toward the fun house at the end of the midway. It loomed ahead of them—a metal facade with a painted mural depicting lovely scenes of murder, mayhem, and decapitation. Scantily clad women ran screaming from gooey, bloody monsters.

This was actually *not* the kind of place that Willow had always dreamed of exploring when it was closed, but she had to back up her lie.

When they got closer to the fun house, she noticed that the entrance was shut and locked with a padlock. "It's locked!" she said cheerfully. "We can't get in."

"Not to worry." With a smile, Lonnie pulled a hefty ring of keys off the belt buckle of his jeans. "I work here, remember?"

He strode toward the fun house in his dusty cowboy boots and climbed the stairs to the entrance, while Willow stood and mentally wrung her hands. She wondered if she should try to escape, but it took only an instant for Lonnie to unlock the padlock.

If I run now, she reasoned, *that will leave Xander alone and unprotected. Well, not exactly alone . . .*

Lonnie pushed the door of the fun house open and motioned toward the darkness. "After you, sweetheart."

CHAPTER 5

Although the sun was shining brightly, Buffy and Giles walked slowly through the cemetery. They could see their destination in the distance, a white spire that towered over the other tombstones and mausoleums. They moved cautiously, not because of vampires or coyotes but because of the police. Two squad cars sat in the parking lot, and Buffy was sure the police were investigating the grave she had visited last night.

Even before they saw the cops, Buffy heard the disembodied voices droning on their radios. She nearly turned back, preferring to wait until after they had left, but she kept walking.

It wasn't that Buffy feared the police, it was just that they were in her way. Most of the time, they didn't believe her when she told them the truth. Of course, if they ever did believe her, they would probably lock her up for sticking wooden stakes in dead people who were still walking around. When it came to the supernatural, the police were extremely dense.

She was relieved to see just two uniformed officers standing near the spire and the molested grave. Withered flowers were strewn all over the gravesite and the surrounding lawn. The cops weren't in heavy investigational mode, with yellow tape blocking off the site and techies crawling all over one another. They were just checking things out.

"I presume that is the grave," Giles whispered. "Should we go down while the police are there?"

"Might as well," Buffy answered. "I want to find out who called them."

The pert Slayer strode ahead of the cautious Watcher, and the two police officers turned to observe her. She strode up to the grave, which was covered with fresh holes that looked as if they had been dug by dogs looking for bones.

"Please stay away, Miss," one of the officers warned. "Crime scene."

"Okay." Before Buffy stepped back, she took a long look at the letters carved into the massive tombstone. The largest letters spelled a strange name—Spurs Hardaway—and there were Wild West sheriff's stars beside his name, as if he was some sort of lawman.

"What happened?" she asked dumbly.

"That's what we're trying to find out," the younger of the two cops answered, giving her a friendly smile.

"It's none of your business," the gray-haired older cop grumbled. "Why don't you just run along?"

Buffy glanced at Giles, who was hiding a smile. He knew she hated it when people were condescending toward her.

"Okay," Buffy said. "I'll go away. But I know exactly who did it."

As she strode away, the two cops staggered up the hill after her. "Wait a minute, Miss! You know about this?" the younger one asked.

"I have a theory," she said teasingly. "You must have some clues. Who called you?"

"The groundskeeper," the older cop answered. "He found the grave all messed up and called us. There's always trouble in this cemetery—I'd like to pave it over."

"Me, too," Buffy muttered.

The cop gave her a quizzical look, then gazed at the grave. "It doesn't look like regular vandalism—more like wild animals were rooting around. So why don't you tell us what *you* know?"

"I think those coyotes did it," Buffy said angrily. "I live nearby, and I've seen a big pack of them running around the cemetery the last few nights."

The young cop snapped his fingers and turned to his partner. "That's got to be it, Joe. We've had a lot of calls about coyotes all this week. You know, it's the dry season, and they come down from the hills looking for water."

Joe nodded sagely. "Yes, I believe we've cracked this case, with the little lady's help. Now we can turn it over to Animal Control."

"If we only knew *why* they tore up the grave," the young cop grumbled.

"Why do I eat doughnuts? Why is the best wrestling on pay-per-view? You don't need a why with coyotes," his partner scoffed. "They're just plain weird."

Buffy peered innocently at the grave again, and Giles edged closer, too. "Is this guy anyone important?" she asked. "Who is Spurs Hardaway?"

The young cop grinned. "Only Joe here is old enough to answer that one."

The old cop scowled. "How quickly they forget. Spurs Hardaway used to be a big Wild West star toward the end of the last century. I mean, he was as big as Buffalo Bill Cody and Annie Oakley. He had a combination Wild West and magic show, which toured all over the world."

"So how come he's buried here?" Buffy asked with amazement. "In Sunnydale?"

The cop shrugged. "I don't know the whole story. I only know he settled here after he retired from show biz. He was already old when he died—shot to death, he was."

"Exactly one hundred years ago," Giles said, looking at the dates on the tombstone.

"Yes, that would be about right," the cop agreed. "It was a big deal back then, this celebrity getting murdered in our little town."

The young cop looked back at the mauled grave. "Maybe the flowers on this grave had been freshly watered, and they were only trying to get a drink."

"More than likely," the older cop agreed.

Hardly likely, Buffy thought. She turned to Giles. "I think we can go now."

"Absolutely!" he said, his eyes gleaming with excitement. Now that he had a ton of things to research, the librarian was happy.

"Thanks for your help!" the younger cop called as they walked away.

"Anytime!" Buffy answered, marveling that the police had actually believed her about something. Instead of being reassuring, this only made her doubt her own theory. What if they really were just coyotes acting like . . . coyotes?

"Buffy, I apologize," Giles said when they got out of earshot of the police. "This case is sufficiently unusual to make me think we should investigate it. After all, anybody who settles down in Sunnydale—near the Hellmouth—is automatically suspicious. First, I'll research Spurs Hardaway, then I'll do more work on skinwalkers and Coyote Moon. I wonder if I should ask Willow to help me."

"Willow!" Buffy's eyes lit up with terror. "Oh my gosh, I left them alone with those major creeps!"

"What creeps?" Giles asked in alarm.

Buffy jogged ahead of him toward the car. "First,

drive me to the carnival, then you can do your research. Come on! There's no telling what nasty stuff is happening to Xander and Willow."

"Oh, dear!" Giles muttered, running to catch up.

In the dark stillness of the fun house, Willow melted into Lonnie's strong arms. She lifted her chin so that their lips could meet, and it was instant polarity—the current flowed from his lips to hers and back through their bodies, molding them together.

I didn't want this to happen, she told herself, *but it's not too bad.* As he kissed her tenderly, she began to lose her regrets. She hadn't been kissed like this since . . . well, never!

What about Xander? the loyal part of her brain reminded her. *Who?* answered the rest of her brain and most of her body.

His kisses moved from Willow's lips down to her neck, and his blond hair brushed against her nose. Suddenly her senses were filled with the earthy smell of Lonnie's hair, and she pulled back a bit in surprise.

But Lonnie's kisses on her neck grew more insistent, and she worried—not that he was a vampire but that he would give her a hickey! As Willow squirmed to get away from him, grimy strings hanging from the ceiling brushed against her face, and she almost screamed.

I'm in a deserted fun house, she told herself, *with a guy who thinks I'm a carnival ride!*

What would Buffy do?

She decided not to knee Lonnie in the groin, but she did pry his lips from her neck and push him firmly away. "Please, Lonnie, no!" she insisted. "I need a break."

He gave her a hurt look. "Hey, honey, you wanted to come in here—when it was dark and deserted, and we were all alone. Remember?"

She nodded breathlessly. "I did, and it was all I expected—very dark, very all alone. Now I'm ready to leave."

With his skilled hands, he gently brushed the hair off her face. "What's your rush? Rose and Xander will be busy for a while."

If he was trying to get her to stay, that was the wrong thing to say. She fought off his hands as she stumbled deeper into the spooky fun house. When her foot brushed against a metal plate, a scream sounded and a hideous creature popped out of a barrel.

"Aaagh!" Willow screeched, frightened out of her wits until she realized that the monster was just another thrill in the fun house.

Lonnie's arms were all around her again, trying to be comforting. "What's the matter, Willow? What's your hang-up?"

"We're just going too fast, that's all," she answered, trying not to whine or whimper. "I mean, I just met you last night."

"And tomorrow night, I could be gone," he said

glumly. "That's the way it is in show business. We don't have much time."

"We'll have to *make* time," she insisted, pushing him away. "You know, like have a few more dates."

"That's great," Lonnie said with a derisive laugh. "I'm working every night, and you want to go out on *dates.*"

"I'm sorry, that's just the way I am. Sort of proper."

Lonnie nodded, and he was once again calm and reasonable. "Okay, Willow, we'll play by your rules. Let's get to know each other first."

She smiled with relief. "That would be nice."

"You've got to come by the carnival every free moment—like tonight after it closes."

"Tonight?" she asked with a gulp.

"After midnight."

Willow tried to sound brave. "Okay, tonight after midnight."

"It'll be our second date," Lonnie said, holding her hands. "We'll get to know each other so well, I'll be like your high school sweetheart."

"Oh, yeah," Willow said with a nervous laugh. *"Him!"*

"And I'll work as hard as I can to make sure the carnival stays in Sunnydale for as long as possible. Maybe a month." He gave her a tender kiss on the cheek, like a true gentleman. "I suppose I should go out there and do some work. Want to watch me oil the Octopus?"

"Sure," Willow answered with false enthusiasm. "Let's oil that sucker."

Lonnie isn't a monster, Willow thought, *just a handsome guy who is used to getting his way with girls.* Deep down, he seemed to respect her, and he genuinely wanted to see her again. Maybe it was unusual to have a date at midnight, but that was the soonest they could get together. At least the summer was no longer boring.

Feeling a new tenderness toward Lonnie, Willow let him hold her hand and guide her through the dark fun house.

Xander stood outside a small, beat-up trailer, listening to thudding and clunking noises as Rose cleaned up her living quarters. For some reason, she wouldn't just let him come in; she had to put things away first. In a way, this was reassuring, because it made her seem more like a regular girl. Nothing else was regular about her.

Rose was worldly, had a great body, and was a terrific kisser. Xander tried not to wonder what she was doing with someone like *him.* There was always the possibility that she thought Buffy was his girlfriend, and since she didn't like Buffy, she was trying to hurt her by stealing her boyfriend. Xander was not going to say or do anything to dissuade her from this notion. If it would help, he would say he was *married* to Buffy.

Even Willow had found a summer romance at the carnival. It was truly a magical place, although it looked better at night under the twirling neon than during the harsh light of day. In the sunlight, the trailers, rides, and booths looked old and grungy, as if they had been touring for centuries.

Xander put these grim thoughts out of his mind and concentrated on happy thoughts. *Maybe the carnival will stay forever, or maybe I can find a way to stay with the carnival—and Rose—forever.*

Suddenly, the door of the trailer creaked open, and Rose stood there, wearing a Japanese silk robe and not much else. His gaze traveled up her tanned, well-shaped legs to the giant dragon splashed across her chest, and he gulped.

"Come in," the dark-haired seductress said.

In his rush, Xander stumbled as he entered an old one-room camper which was even stranger than he could have imagined. There were prints and paintings on every inch of the walls, shelves full of strange animal figurines, a big wooden sea chest, a tiny bed, and what looked like a torture chamber in the corner. Or maybe it was an ancient dentist's chair. Whatever it was, the corroded needles and tubes didn't look very inviting.

On top of this, the smoke of heavily scented incense floated around Rose's cramped quarters. Xander tried not to cough, but finally he could hold it no longer—he burst out with a large hack.

"Poor boy," Rose said with amusement. "Can't stand a little smoke? The incense will clear your senses."

"My senses have never been clearer!" Xander

croaked. Now he knew where Rose got her husky voice. He lurched forward through the smoke and banged his foot on the big sea chest. "Ow!" he groaned. "What's in this thing, an anchor?"

When he touched the dark wood and brass fittings, Rose bolted to her feet with fire in her eyes. "Don't touch that chest!"

"Sorry," Xander said, backing up and bumping into a shelf of pewter dragons, bears, and wolves. He knocked several of them onto the floor with a clatter.

"Sorry," he said again, even more sheepishly. He reached down to pick up the figurines.

"Just leave them," Rose ordered with exasperation. She sank onto her tiny mattress, which was built more for her petite frame than Xander's. "Come sit over here, it's safer."

When she patted the edge of her bed, Xander was there like a guided missile. "Nice bed," he gushed. "I mean, nice place! Nice *everything!*"

"It's home," she said with a shrug. "The towns change around us, but my lair stays the same."

"Your lair," Xander echoed with a laugh. He looked around with amazement. "It is almost like a cave."

"Isn't it, though."

"How long have you been doing this?" Xander asked. He quickly added, "I mean, traveling with the carnival."

"A long time." She squeezed his shoulders as if he were a side of beef. "I'm older than I look."

He gave a high-pitched giggle at her tickling fingers, then tried to compose himself. "Well, you look great, no matter how old you are."

"Take your shirt off," she ordered.

"Shirt. Okay!" Xander said enthusiastically. He fumbled with the buttons, couldn't get them open, and ended up ripping the shirt off his own back. Then he grinned stupidly at her. "I never did like that shirt."

"You're so funny," she said, studying his naked back and shoulders. "Now, where do you want your tattoo?"

Xander blinked at her. "Tattoo?" From the corner of his eye, he again noticed the archaic tubes and needles on the contraption in the corner. *Uh-oh.*

"I want to brand you, you know," she said with a wink. "Show everyone that you're *mine.*"

"Uh, what kind of tattoo am I going to get?" Xander asked, trying to stall for time.

"A rose, of course."

"Of course!" He laughed nervously. "I've seen your rose tattoo. I suppose you have more than that?"

"Oh, many. Would you like to see them?"

"Yes," Xander rasped, trying not to drool.

She teasingly touched his nose with a lacquered red fingernail. "I bet you would. But you can't see most of them until you get to know me better. Here's a little one you can see."

Rose lifted the hem of her silky robe and showed

him a tattoo of a scorpion high on her hip. Her tan went all the way up, and she didn't appear to be wearing any underwear.

"Nice," Xander breathed. The incense and Rose were both doing a job on him—his senses were on overload.

As he reached to touch the scorpion, she dropped the hem of her robe and pointed to her ankle, where there was a tiny blue star. "I love that little star," she said. "And you should see my moon."

"And . . . and where is that?"

"Where a moon ought to be." Rose winked at him, stood, and crossed to the tattoo machine in the corner. "You didn't tell me where you wanted your tattoo."

"Uh, well—" Xander gulped and rose uneasily to his feet. "You know, I really hadn't thought too much about getting a tattoo—until now. I think I should study them, look at some books, and think about all the possible places you could put one."

He grinned. "Maybe if I saw more of *your* tattoos, that would inspire me."

Rose sauntered back to him and wrapped her arms around his neck. She pulled him tantalizingly close to her. "You're a smart boy, aren't you? You're not going to give something for nothing. You *will* belong to Rose, whether you wear her brand or not."

"That's okay with me," Xander said heavily, his lips almost touching hers.

"The carnival closes at midnight," she whispered. "Come back and meet me, and you'll see the stars, the moon . . . and everything else."

"Midnight," he muttered as his lips eagerly found hers.

Xander tried to control himself, but he kissed like a man in a vacuum chamber, gasping for air. He wanted to consume her, to drink her, to *breathe* her! Nothing was ever so wonderful as her embrace, especially when she pressed her body against his and ran her fingernails through his hair. Just when he thought he could stand no more, the door banged open.

Both of them jumped with surprise, and they turned to see an ominous figure standing in the doorway, silhouetted in bright sunlight. Xander was reminded of old westerns, when the hero strides into a saloon to clean out the bad guys.

"Buffy!" he gasped. "What are you doing here?"

She ignored him and strode right up to Rose. "Okay, Thorny, turn him loose."

"He's mine now," Rose declared. She dropped her hands and balled them into fists.

Xander quickly grabbed her hands and tried to put them back on his neck. "No, no, don't turn me loose! Hold on to me. I might get away!"

But the mood was broken, as Buffy and Rose glared laser beams at each other. *Gosh,* Xander thought, *things could be worse. They're both beautiful, and they're fighting over me!*

"That's all right, ladies, there's plenty enough to go around," he assured them. *But, Buffy, why don't you split now—I'm on a date,* he tried to tell her with his eyes.

The Slayer never took her eyes off Rose. "Xander, there's something I've got to tell you about these people. Can you wait outside?"

"*You* wait outside!" Rose snapped, pushing Buffy toward the door. When the Slayer dropped into her fighting stance, Xander feared that Rose would get a mouthful of feet.

"Oh, are you going to do some kung fu on me?" the carny asked with a laugh. "I think you watch too much TV."

"Don't get into a fight with her!" Xander warned.

"I'm already in a fight with her." Rose whirled around in a lightning-fast motion and slugged Buffy, sending her tumbling out the door into the dusty midway.

While Buffy writhed on her back, Rose sprang out of the trailer and landed on her throat, snarling like a wild animal. It took every ounce of Buffy's strength to keep the dark-haired woman's teeth from her throat, but the Slayer finally pushed her off and rolled free.

Both women jumped to their feet and circled each other warily. Fortunately, the carnival was still closed, so there weren't any witnesses to this fight, except for Xander.

"Come on, Buffy," Xander pleaded. "You're taking this thing too far! Fighting doesn't solve anything. If only you had told me how you felt about me, and that you were so jealous—"

"Jealous?" Buffy asked in amazement. "Xander, I only wanted to talk to you for a second."

"You couldn't leave me a message on my *answering machine?"* he wailed.

Rose finally doubled over, laughing. "You two are a real pair! It's been fun, Xander, but I've got to go to work. If you want to ditch this confused teenybopper for a real woman, you know where to find me, and what time." With that, Rose stalked into her trailer and slammed the door shut behind her.

"Confused teenybopper?" Buffy muttered angrily.

"You *are* confused!" Xander shouted, waving his arms in exasperation. "And you're acting like a teenybopper. First you bust into Rose's trailer, assault my date, and then you say it was for *no reason!"*

Buffy lowered her voice. "I did it to save you."

"Save me!" he shrieked. "You saved me from the one thing in the world I *least* want to be saved from!"

"Your love life is not the issue," Buffy said. "Your life—"

"My life? These people have been real nice to me and Willow. And they haven't done anything to you! Sure, maybe they try to make a few bucks from the locals, but that makes them *normal!* You're the only one who's acting crazy around here. These people are not monsters."

Buffy grabbed his sleeve. "Come with me to the library. Let's sit down with Giles and—"

"The only monster is *you!*" Xander snapped, yanking his arm away from her. "It's not part of your job description to ruin my dates."

He stormed off toward the midway, and Buffy chased after him. "When are you supposed to see her again?"

Xander covered his ears. "I'm not hearing you—you're not here!"

"Where's Willow?"

"I don't know, and I wouldn't tell you even if I did know!" He turned and glared at her. "You didn't want me, Buffy, so mellow out."

As Xander stalked off, Buffy stood dumbfounded in the middle of the deserted carnival. *Boy, I sure messed that up.* Not only had she failed to save Xander, but she had driven him toward the enemy. Of course, the enemy was shapely and pretty, so it didn't take much to lose Xander. Even if she found Willow, she doubted she could make her believe that the carnies were really werecoyotes.

The only real evidence she had was a chewed-up dog collar. The rest of it was just hunches and gut instinct. It was even possible that she was wrong, in which case she may have lost a good friend for nothing.

Could Xander be right? Was part of her reaction caused by jealousy? Being cute and cuddly, Buffy had always taken boys for granted, and that was fine in her previous life. Since becoming the Slayer, however, her love life had gone down the garbage disposal. Normally, this strengthened her bond with Willow and Xander, who were hopeless in romance for other reasons—but since the carnival they had suddenly gotten hot love lives. All Buffy had was a weird, majorly dangerous job whose pay stank.

She took a deep breath and tried to squelch the feeling-sorry-for-herself routine. Fighting evil had to be its own reward. Even though she had alienated one of her best friends, Buffy had learned one thing: Rose was unusually strong for a human. Her strength and agility made her a match for Buffy, or even a vampire. Once again, that was a nice thing to know, but it didn't prove anything.

The Slayer brushed the dust off her shirt and hip-huggers, then began to stroll nonchalantly out of the carnival. When she had entered, there were a handful of carnies working and hanging out—she had asked one of them how to get to Rose's trailer. Now they were gone, except for one.

Hopscotch, the man with the coyote eyes, stood watching her from the deck of the Tilt-a-Whirl. His craggy face looked full of suspicion and disappointed at the same time, and he was wiping his hands on a grimy rag. Buffy felt like asking him a few questions, but she had picked enough fights for one day. She put her head down and hurried on her way.

Maybe Giles would have some answers.

CHAPTER 6

Buffy wandered into the darkened school library and found Giles hunched over a table full of old books. Only one small desk lamp was turned on, and he had six books open underneath it. His nose was buried inside a large coffee-table book full of colorful paintings, and he was rapidly scribbling notes.

"Hi," she said, causing him to lift his chin and finally acknowledge her presence.

"Hello!" he answered cheerfully. "Spurs Hardaway turns out to be a fascinating character—just the sort of person to live in Sunnydale. Um, how are Xander and Willow?"

"They're fabulous, I guess." Buffy shrugged and slumped into a chair across the table from him. "Xander's mad at me, and Willow's disappeared. Even her mother doesn't know where she is—only

...on't be home until late tonight. Of course, ...er one of them wants to hear anything from *...e.*"

"What do you mean?" Giles asked in alarm.

"I mean, we can't count on them this time. They're on the other side, giving aid and comfort to the enemy."

Giles nodded thoughtfully. "I presume you still think that the carnival workers are the werecoyotes?"

"Yes, but I don't have any proof, except for a dog collar," Buffy muttered. "Xander is really ga-ga over his carnival babe, and Willow is in the clutches of a super-hunk with lots of smooth lines."

She could tell that Giles was trying to phrase his next remark delicately. "You seem awfully certain about this, but it is *possible* that the carnival folk are harmless."

Buffy rolled her eyes. "You haven't met them. Even if they're not werecoyotes, they're far from harmless."

"But that's a decision Xander and Willow should make for themselves."

"Duh! I know everybody thinks I'm playing Mrs. Brady, but I know what I know . . . or what I feel." Buffy tossed her honey-blond hair. "Enough about Xander and Willow—what did you find out?"

"This will give you some idea of how popular Spurs Hardaway was." Giles picked up the coffee-table book he was reading and set it in front of her.

Buffy had thought it was a book of paintings, but now that she got a closer look, she saw that it was a collection of old theatrical posters.

On the left page was a colorful painting depicting a long-haired mountain man surrounded by wolves, buffaloes, bears, and mountain lions. Below this was a scene of Indians on horseback circling a flaming covered wagon.

Banner headlines on the poster proclaimed, "Spurs Hardaway and the Thrilling Magic of the Wild West! Witness the Vicious Indian Attack! Gasp at Animals Never Before Seen in New York! Relive the Magic and Romance of the West!"

On the right page was another heroic portrait of Spurs Hardaway, this time wrestling a bear. Below that was an illustration of what looked like a rodeo parade, with lots of bespangled cowboys and Indians. At the bottom of the page was a scene of Spurs and a mountain lion inside a golden cage. But the writing on this poster was all in French.

"That's from his triumphant European tour in 1889," Giles said, pointing to the French poster. "By all accounts, Spurs Hardaway put on a magnificent show, with a cast of more than two hundred cowboys and wild animals. It was a combination rodeo, stuntman, circus, and magic act."

"So he was the Siegfried and Roy of his day."

"Who? Listen to this—his most famous magic trick was to climb into a cage, have the cage covered with a velvet curtain, and then turn himself into a wild animal! There are eyewitness accounts of Hardaway turning himself into a wolf, a mountain lion, and a bear."

Buffy narrowed her eyes at the Watcher. "Just because he did that trick doesn't mean he *really* turned into a wolf or a bear."

"Au contraire," Giles answered triumphantly. "Spurs Hardaway claimed that he really *could* turn himself into a wild animal, a trick he said he learned from the Plains Indians. At the time, his critics dismissed this claim as mere publicity, but what if he were telling the truth? We know that skinwalkers exist, and there were reportedly other performers in his troupe who could turn themselves into animals."

"Wow," Buffy said, getting a queasy feeling in her stomach. "But it could still be a trick—magicians do it today."

Giles shook his head. "Not like Spurs Hardaway did it. He did this trick everywhere—in circus tents, stadiums, saloons, even in jail cells. Turning oneself into a bear or a wolf is not a simple trick—you need a proper theater with a stage that has a trap door. Do you remember the badges on his tombstone?"

"Yes."

"In his youth, Spurs Hardaway was an Army scout and a federal marshal, and he spent many years living among the Indians. That was before they learned to be wary of white men."

"So he took Skinwalking 101," Buffy said. "But what is his connection to Sunnydale?"

"In 1895, he retired here, although his Wild West show kept touring without him. In fact, Spurs owned a great deal of land in the area—he was one of the founding fathers of Sunnydale. Suspicious, isn't it? I think he knew that he was right on top of a tremendous source of occult energy, although he may not have known how to access it."

"But he was mortal. He did die."

"Yes, and that's highly suspicious, too." Giles paused for dramatic effect. "On his eighty-first birthday, Spurs was shot to death in his home—with a silver bullet. His murderer was never caught."

Buffy rose to her feet and began to pace. "You know, it's not much of a leap from being in a Wild West show to being in a carnival. City after city. Bad food after cheap food. Sawdust. Stuffed animals. It's the same kind of job, really, only the scam is different. Suppose the carnies are his followers from way back when, and they're still touring. Only now they can't do a Wild West show—p.c. police and all—so they have to do a cheesy carnival."

"It makes sense," Giles agreed.

Buffy frowned. "No, it doesn't. Most of them are too young. They're hardly older than me."

"Not necessarily," Giles said. "They could derive tremendous power from skinwalking. Throughout the ages, shape-shifting has been regarded as an advanced shamanistic skill. Anybody who has mastered it has undoubtedly mastered other spells, and the ability to look young could be one of them.

When he died, Spurs Hardaway was said to look no older than a man of forty, even though he was eighty-one."

The Watcher's jaw clenched in anger. "They've taken a formidable power from the Native Americans and have completely perverted it. It's possible that they could be very skilled sorcerers."

"And they keep their secret safe by living in a carnival," Buffy added. "Always on the move, going from town to town—so nobody knows that they never grow old."

"Exactly! But they are mortal. We know that they can be killed by the traditional silver projectile."

Buffy frowned at that notion as she continued to pace. "Yeah, I know we could kill them, but they aren't exactly vampires. I mean, they aren't running around ripping people's throats open. They attacked *me,* but that's because they know I'm onto them. Otherwise, they've only done small stuff, minor vandalism."

"Are you saying, after all this urgency, that these werecoyotes aren't dangerous?"

"That all depends. As carnies, they'll take your money and seduce your friends," Buffy said bitterly. "As coyotes, they'll eat your dog and dig up an old grave—but we can't *kill* them for any of that. We can't even go to the police, without giving them a good laugh."

Giles pushed his glasses up the bridge of his nose. "I see what you mean. They have behaved badly, but not that badly. Plus, there's the irksome problem that we don't have any proof."

"If only we knew why they're back here in Sunnydale. Why now? What were they doing in the cemetery last night, looking for bones in their old boss's grave?"

The Watcher suddenly looked grim. "There's one thing I forgot to tell you—about Coyote Moon. I did some calculations, and *tonight* is a Coyote Moon. Also, it's exactly one hundred years since Spurs Hardaway was murdered. Perhaps, like a vampire, he can be resurrected one hundred years after his death."

Buffy let out a low breath. "Last night, the freaky coyotes did look like they were doing some kind of ceremony."

"We'll never know if any of these theories are true, unless we observe them firsthand or find irrefutable evidence."

"Coyote skins," the Slayer said. "If we're right, each one of them has to have his own coyote skin. I've got to find out for sure."

"*We've* got to find out," Giles said forcefully. "I insist upon coming with you. There's no more useful research I can do here, and four eyes are better than two."

She pointed to his glasses and smiled. "You should know."

"What can we bring? I may have a few silver bullets in the weapons locker."

Buffy winced. "Let's try not to kill any of them, okay? Some of them are kind of cute. Besides, if we can get proof, at least we can tell Willow and Xander to stay away from them."

She gazed worriedly out the window and saw the burning embers of sunset stretching across the sky. "I only hope Willow and Xander are all right."

"Ante up, boys," Willow said, forming her gigantic pile of poker chips into several neat stacks. The tiny trailer was smoky with tobacco and incense, but Willow figured she had won about two hundred dollars from the carnies so far. She could stand the smoke a little while longer, if they could stand the heat.

She shuffled the deck. "Shall we keep it five-card draw, deuces and one-eyed jacks wild?"

"How are you winning so much?" Lonnie grumbled. "You didn't tell me you were a poker shark."

Willow grinned. "Well, I do quite well against my family when we're playing for Monopoly money. I guess that skill carries over into real money. Poker is a mathematical game, after all, with probabilities and risk factors that can be calculated. Money management is also important."

An old carny with strange, rheumy eyes scowled and picked up his pathetic handful of chips. "Cash me out. I can't beat this poker witch! Next time, Lonnie, don't bring no ringers into the game."

"Hey, Hopscotch, I didn't know!" the blond-haired hunk insisted. "I loaned her five bucks so she could play a few hands. Who knew?"

Willow cheerfully counted the old man's chips and gave him $3.75. "It was a pleasure meeting you."

"Right," he grumbled. "I'm going outside to keep a lookout for that vandal before we open up."

"You have a vandal?" Willow asked in alarm.

The old man gave her a sneer. "Just someone who wants to screw things up for us. We'll catch 'em."

"Why don't you tell the police?"

Hopscotch rubbed the gray stubble on his chin. "We don't hold with outsiders knowing our business. In the carnival, we have our own brand of justice."

"I see," Willow said with a nervous smile.

"Come on, *deal!*" growled one of the players, a bare-chested young carny with long dark hair. Hopscotch waved and ambled out the door.

"You didn't ante up," Willow said, and the young man scowled and tossed two fifty-cent chips into the pile. Willow shuffled the cards and dealt to him, Lonnie, a third carny, and herself. She decided not to be so ruthless; maybe she would even give them some of their money back.

"Remind me never to play strip poker with you," Lonnie said with a wink.

Willow blushed. "Okay, I won't let it cross your mind."

"We might as well be playing strip poker," the guy

without a shirt muttered. "Any more hands like this, and I'll be lucky to have my underwear."

"I can only give you fifty cents for your underwear," Willow joked. "I think that's more than generous."

Lonnie laughed. "I'll give you two cents."

Still smiling, Willow picked up her cards and saw two queens and a two, which was a wild card. Even before drawing any more cards, she already had three queens. *No sense denying it,* Willow thought cheerfully, *it's my lucky day.*

Xander snored loudly as he lay in his bed, sleeping through dinner. He had asked his mother not to wake him—not even for food—because he had a date planned and he needed to rest up for it. As he grinned in peaceful slumber, Xander dreamed of blue tattoos on creamy brown skin.

When Buffy and Giles strolled into the carnival at sunset, it seemed like a ghost town just coming to life after a long slumber. One by one, the neon lights twinkled on, and the towering machines grumbled to life. With creaks and groans, the mighty arms of the Octopus and the Ferris wheel began to rotate, lighting up the sky with sweeping rainbows of color. French fries, corn dogs, and fry bread bubbled in vats of grease, lending a homey smell to the air. Surfer music blared from crackling speakers.

It was as if every night were the same, just a continuation of the night before.

Buffy noticed families with children roaming around the kiddie rides, but most of them would be gone in another hour or so. The carnival after dark was a world of young people, shady people, and night people. Giles stood beside Buffy, gaping at the gaudy attractions and the milling crowd of teenagers.

"Oh, my," Giles muttered. "Western civilization is in more trouble than I thought."

Buffy sighed. "Well, nobody forces the kids to come here. We do it of our own free will."

"Terrifying," Giles agreed. "So where do we begin searching in this den of depravity?"

Buffy lowered her voice. "Time for a fashion check. I'm afraid we have to sneak into somebody's trailer, as I don't think they carry their coyote skins in their back pockets. I know where Rose's trailer is, but first let's see if she's working at the moment."

With Buffy leading the way, they strode down the midway, ignoring the barkers who kept trying to lure them into rides and games. She kept her eyes open for Hopscotch, who was probably spying on her from the shadows, but she didn't see the old carny. Perhaps he was actually working tonight, since there was a big crowd and all the rides were whirling at once.

As they walked, Giles gaped at the rides, the games, the food stands, and the people. When he saw a young girl eating a huge spool of blue cotton candy, he followed her for several strides. Buffy had to grab his arm and drag him back into the real world.

"Did you see what she was eating?" Giles asked in amazement. "It looked like . . . like ectoplasm!"

"What's ectoplasm?" Buffy asked.

"The nebulous material from which ghosts are made."

"Oh, it *tastes* like ectoplasm, too," Buffy said. "Only with lots of sugar."

"It can't be good for you," Giles concluded.

"Does any of this look like it's good for you? This is one of those places where you can be a kid and an adult at the same time. That's why teens love it."

Squinting through his glasses, Giles surveyed a row of busy game booths. "I see what you mean about the carnival workers looking rather young and fit, but perhaps that's not unusual. Traveling all the time, living off the land—this would be an occupation for young, fit people."

"I know!" Buffy snapped with frustration. "And maybe it's a coincidence that there's a pack of coyotes running rampant in Sunnydale at the same time. Maybe it's a coincidence that they were digging up Spurs Hardaway's grave, and that he died a hundred years ago today. That's why we have to convince *ourselves* of what's going on before we can convince anyone else."

"Is that your real hair?" a voice barked over a loudspeaker, "or are you wearing a muskrat on your head?"

"We're here." Buffy held out her hand and stopped Giles as they neared the dunking machine.

The same clown she had dunked last night was on

duty, and he was making fun of an older man wearing a toupee. Also on duty was his partner, the dark-haired vixen Rose. As usual, she was exchanging soggy softballs and sexy pouts for crisp dollar bills, while making fools out of a long line of men.

"Xander's new girlfriend is hard at work," Buffy said.

Giles peered through his glasses. "*That* is the young . . . woman who is interested in Xander?"

"See what I mean?" Buffy asked. "That's just one too many coincidences. Last night, it seemed as if all the carnies were trying to pick up local kids."

"Onerous behavior, to be sure," Giles said, "but they could be normal lowlifes instead of shape-shifting lowlifes. Unless they commit a crime or we can get proof of what they are, we really can't do anything."

"So let's get our proof." Buffy steered the librarian toward the rides, away from the dunking machine. Taking a circuitous route to the rear of the carnival, they wound up behind the neon lights and painted facades. Back here, the paint was chipped on the beat-up trailers, noisy generators, and smelly garbage cans. It was like the dark slum hidden away from the warm city lights.

With Rose's nondescript trailer in sight, Buffy and Giles crept through the shadows. Hearing voices, they crouched down behind a pile of lumber. They listened warily as two teenagers walked past, taking a shortcut to the parking lot.

"Okay," Buffy whispered. "You stay out here and

do what you do—watch—while I go inside. If anybody looks like they're coming to the trailer, knock on the side, then split. I'll get away as best I can, and we'll meet back at your car. Okay?"

Giles gulped and nodded. "I was just thinking that we could be arrested for this."

"Somehow, I don't think this group is big on calling the police. Here goes." Buffy stood and tried the door of the trailer. It was locked, so she grabbed the door handle and snapped it off, as if it was a dried twig. The door of the tiny trailer swung open, and she had to duck to enter.

Once inside, Buffy thought about putting on a light, but she could see fairly well. Through a grimy window, the swirling neon rides splashed a kaleidoscope of colors onto the opposite wall. It was just enough light to see by.

Buffy tried to ignore the weird smell, which was either incense or Rose's cheap perfume. Her eyes scanned the cluttered walls and shelves, but she didn't think that Rose's coyote skin would be hanging in plain sight. *I could never live in this tiny trailer,* Buffy thought. *There isn't any closet space.*

When her eyes hit upon the old wooden sea chest, she knew it was the only possible hiding place for the skin. She bent down to open the trunk and discovered that it had a strong padlock holding the clasp shut. If she had all the time in the world, she could probably loosen the lock without anyone knowing it, but she didn't have all the time in the world. Every second counted.

Buffy gripped the case in one hand and the shackle in the other and pulled the lock apart with a loud *sproing.* A small spring shot across the room, and the lock crumbled to pieces in her hands.

The lid of the old sea chest creaked loudly as she lifted it, and she plunged her hands into the silky contents. It seemed to be full of clothes—only they weren't clothes exactly, more like fancy costumes with fringe and sequins. *Maybe Rose moonlights as a go-go girl,* Buffy thought. Her fingers dug deeper into the pile of fancy clothes, looking for only one thing.

She finally touched it deep at the bottom—the greasy fur of an old pelt! Just as she was about to pull it out and inspect it, a frantic pounding sounded on the wall of the trailer. That was Giles's signal—somebody was coming! Buffy hoped that the Watcher would get away, but she was not about to leave without her prize, her proof.

Then she heard another sound, even closer. From somewhere at the back of the trailer came a low, rumbling growl. The animal could be a coyote, but it sounded bigger—much bigger. And *inside* the trailer.

A shadow loomed in front of her as the unseen beast lunged for her throat!

CHAPTER 7

With no time to think, Buffy lifted the chest and used it as a shield, and the snarling beast crashed into it, splintering the wood and knocking Buffy backward. As slinky go-go outfits cascaded all around them, Buffy and the monster rolled on the floor. She fought to keep the pieces of the chest between them, but the beast was strong and determined. No matter what she did, she felt its hot breath on her throat.

With a karate cry, she punched the creature in its thick, furry neck, causing it to yelp with pain. Keeping on the offensive, Buffy kept punching and kicking until she propelled the beast away from her, then she rolled to her feet and dove out the door.

When she looked up from the ground, she saw four pairs of legs surrounding her. Rough hands grabbed her and dragged her to her feet, and Buffy recognized most of the carnies: Lonnie, Hopscotch, Rose, and the guy who ran the basketball booth. She looked worriedly behind her, but the ferocious beast that had attacked her was nowhere in sight.

Rose, however, looked really ticked off. "That's *twice* today you've broken into my trailer!"

With a swift motion, Rose swung her fist and buried it in Buffy's midsection. After the fight with the beast, she was tired. As the air rushed out of Buffy's lungs, she slumped to the ground—she was such dead weight that the three guys couldn't hold her up. They dropped her into the dust. For several seconds, Buffy could do nothing but gasp for air.

"And you!" Rose said accusingly. "You're supposed to be protecting my place. What happened?"

From the corner of her eye, Buffy saw Rose addressing a four-legged creature standing well inside the doorway of her trailer. It wasn't a mystery beast—it was a big, black dog—husky, like a rottweiler. She had been attacked by a watchdog, not a watchmonster.

"He did his job," Buffy groaned. "He caught me by surprise."

"What *is* your problem, anyway?" Lonnie muttered, turning her over with the point of his boot. "What are you looking for, besides trouble?"

"My boyfriend—" Buffy answered, hoping they would believe her.

"That's bull!" Rose snapped. "He's not here, and you know it. You were snooping around again."

"What should we do with her?" Hopscotch asked, pushing painfully on her shoulder.

Lonnie knelt down so that his eyes were level with Buffy's. "Listen to me, you little snoop. You stay away from us, starting right now, or you'll never see your friends again."

Buffy glared at him, knowing he could probably make good on that threat. She thought about trying to escape, but she wasn't in any condition to put up much of a fight. "Why don't you go chase your tail? Or scratch your fleas?" she asked. "We have enough trouble in this town without your kind."

"And what is *our* kind?" Lonnie asked with a sneer. It was as if he was daring her to say what she suspected about them. Well, Buffy wasn't going to fall into that trap. She was gathering information, not giving it out.

"Listen, call the police on me if you want," Buffy said defiantly. "If you're not going to do that, turn me loose."

Lonnie smiled, looking again like the charming ladies' man she had met the night before. "Buffy—that's your name, right? You know, Buffy, I think you got us all wrong. We're just young kids, not long out of school, just trying to make a living and see some of the world. As for Willow and Xander, why don't you relax and let them have some fun? They're here of their own free will."

"Is that important?" Buffy asked.

Lonnie scowled and rose to his feet. "I don't know

what we should do with her. Maybe we should lock her up somewhere until . . . after."

"Watch her, she's awfully strong," Rose warned with a knowing glance at Buffy. She shoved her dog back into the trailer and tried to lock the door. "She broke my lock clean off."

"I've got a safe place for her," Hopscotch suggested. "The big tool chest in the utility rig. She should just about fit."

"I don't want to be kidnapped!" Buffy said, pretending to struggle. She stared at Rose. "Just let me go home—you can have my stupid boyfriend!"

Rose chuckled. "Thanks. I've already got him. And I have big plans for him, too."

Lonnie looked at Hopscotch and nodded. Buffy should have reacted quicker, but she was still trying to get her wind back. She didn't see the wrench in Hopscotch's hand until it came flying through the air, cracking onto the back of her head.

As blackness and pain engulfed her senses, Buffy slumped face-first into the dirt.

Giles paced in front of his car, wondering what had become of Buffy. Had she been caught inside the trailer? Had they called the police on her? Now he felt guilty about giving the signal and running off, but he had only been following her orders. She was the Slayer—always risking her life in order to keep other people safe. He feared that someday that policy might backfire on her.

He checked his watch and saw that it had been

twenty minutes since he had left Buffy inside the trailer. She had said they would meet at his car, but that presupposed that both of them were coming. Buffy was obviously not coming, at least not quickly.

A young couple walked by, and they glanced at him suspiciously, as if thinking: *What is this middle-aged guy in a tie doing hanging out in the parking lot of a carnival?* Giles smiled reassuringly at them, and they hurried along their way. *Maybe I should be more inconspicuous,* he decided. He unlocked the door of his car and climbed behind the steering wheel.

But ten minutes of sitting in the car only made him more nervous than before. He didn't like sitting in the car, because he couldn't *see* anything. *What if Buffy forgot where the car was parked? What if she's wandering around, looking for it?*

Giles jumped out and started pacing in front of his car again. He scanned the swirling lights of the carnival for any sign of the perky teenager. Every other teenager in town seemed to be in attendance at the gaudy attractions, but not Buffy.

After a few minutes, Giles took a handkerchief out of his pocket and wiped the sweat off his neck. As he did, he surveyed the dark hills behind the vacant lot, and he saw something even more disturbing. The full moon had just started to rise, and it glowed blood-red in the night sky.

Coyote Moon!

Even though they had no real proof of the existence of werecoyotes or a plot to resurrect Spurs Hardaway, the sight of the moon filled Giles with dread. Bold and bright, it seemed to challenge the very lights of the carnival. By midnight, it would be fully risen in the night sky, and it would be bone-white. Giles found it hard to watch the red moon without thinking that evil was abroad on this hot summer's night.

Now forty minutes had passed since he had left Buffy inside the trailer, and that was more than enough time to wait for her. Giles resolved to disobey orders and go look for her, starting with Rose's trailer.

Two minutes later, he was once again in the shadows behind the midway, stalking Rose's darkened trailer. Nothing appeared amiss—it looked exactly as he had left it. As if he owned the place, Giles walked briskly to the door and tried the handle. The lock was broken, but the door had been wired shut with a metal clothes hanger.

Without warning, something large crashed against the door on the other side, barking and growling ferociously. Giles staggered away from the trailer, nearly falling into the dirt, as the beast inside continued to growl and carry on. *Whatever is in there,* he thought, *it isn't human, and it isn't Buffy!*

He looked around, worried that the loud barking would surely draw a crowd. No one came to investigate, but still he scurried away, feeling cowardly and helpless.

Back on the brightly lit midway, Giles wandered for a while, looking for Buffy, Willow, or Xander. All he saw were the callow youths of Sunnydale and the creepy youths who ran the carnival. He did pass two uniformed police officers, who were drinking coffee and eating huge cinnamon rolls, but what could he tell them?

Excuse me, Officer, one of my students has disappeared while breaking into a locked trailer, looking for proof of werecoyotes.

No, Buffy had gotten herself into whatever trouble she had gotten herself into, and she would have to get herself out. Giles tried to tell himself that she was the Slayer—she would know what to do. But these weren't garden-variety vampires, such as those she had fought dozens of times—these were sorcerers, shape-shifters! They were potentially more powerful than vampires.

Giles kept walking through the carnival, determined not to leave until he found Buffy.

Buffy awoke with a massive headache clamped to her skull like a baby alien. She was either in total darkness or she was blind. When she squirmed painfully, trying to work out the kinks, she discovered that she was trapped inside a thick metal box about two feet by four feet.

As terror overcame her, Buffy tried to struggle and shout. She didn't get far, because her hands were tied behind her back and her mouth was taped shut. About all she could do was kick her feet against the sides of the box, which seemed as solid as a steel coffin.

Buffy kicked and kicked, until she was gasping for breath. She stopped, thinking that she had to be careful or she would use up all the air in this small enclosure. Buffy smelled oil and grease, which she assumed were all over her clothes and hair by now. *Great! Now I'll need a pro-vitamin mud treatment to even begin to restore my hair.* Of course, that wouldn't matter much if she died in this metal crypt.

Worse yet, she had failed Giles, Willow, Xander, and all the other local kids who were in danger. She had failed to stop the werecoyotes, who were now free to have a coming-out party for Spurs Hardaway. That dog in the trailer—it might not have been a dog at all but a man wearing a dog skin! With this scary gang of skinwalkers, there was no telling what was real and what wasn't.

She began kicking ferociously on the side of the box as she squirmed to free herself. All of this frenzied activity made her throbbing headache worse, but she wasn't going to just lie here and die—

Bang! Bang! came two loud raps on the wall of her prison. "Quiet down in there!" a muffled voice shouted.

Buffy stopped thrashing, but she continued to work quietly on the ropes binding her wrists. Unfortunately, she had been tied up by strong people who knew their way around ropes and knots. In her awkward position, she couldn't exert much force on the ropes, and she couldn't budge them.

With her lips, tongue, and teeth, Buffy began to work on the tape spread across her mouth. She had always wondered whether her tongue had extraordinary strength, too, and apparently it did. Very slowly, she worked the tape down from her upper lip until she had a small gap through which she could talk.

"Let me out of here!" she yelled.

The banging came again. "Shut up in there!"

"No!"

A moment later, the lid of the box opened, and the silhouette of a man looked down at her. "Listen," he hissed, "I could fix you so that you'll never talk again! All it takes is a little snip-snip on your tongue. But if you promise not to yell and cause a ruckus, I'll take off the gag. Believe it or not, Missy, I *want* to talk to you."

Buffy recognized the voice—she was pretty sure it was Hopscotch. She wasn't in much of a position to bargain, so she nodded and mumbled, "Okay, I'll keep quiet."

He lowered the lid, plunging her back into darkness. She had no reason to trust the old carny, but there had been a weird desperation in his voice, as if he, too, needed help. At least, by opening the top of the box, he had let some much-needed fresh air into the box and her lungs. The fresh air even helped clear her headache a little bit.

To her relief, the top of the box opened again a few minutes later. This time, Hopscotch had a flashlight, which he shined into her face. She closed her eyes and didn't see his big hand coming down to her mouth, until he ripped the tape off her lips. Buffy yelped.

"Sorry," he muttered.

"Yeah, thanks. Now I won't have to wax my mustache for a while."

"Hey, nobody forced you to snoop around."

Buffy sighed. "I shouldn't have broken into that trailer, I know it now—but love makes you do silly things! Why don't you just let me go, and we'll forget all about that, and the fact that you kidnapped me?"

"Are you *really* just a lovesick teenager?" Hopscotch asked with a suspicious glint in his eye.

Some instinct told Buffy not to lie. "No," she answered. "I mean, Xander is a friend of mine, but I'm more worried about his *life* than his love life."

"You're smart," Hopscotch said with respect. "You *see* things. I remember you from that first night—there was something about you."

"You don't mean that first night when we met here, do you?" Buffy asked.

"No, when I met you on the street, when I was running with the pack. The others think all humans are worthless fools, but not me. After all, *we* were once human."

Bingo! she thought. "You guys are werecoyotes—skinwalkers."

Hopscotch chuckled. "Hoo-boy, you got it all

figured out! We've been roaming this country for a century now, and nobody's guessed our game until *you* came along. You can fight, too. I still got bruises from where you kicked me the other night. So what's *your* story, Missy?"

"Since we're friends now, why don't you let me out of here? Then we can sit around and have a regular conversation."

He shoved the flashlight in her face. "Tell me what you are, or I'll shut you up permanently."

"Okay," Buffy said, wincing from the light. "I'm a . . . a witch! I run this town, and I don't want any competition."

Hopscotch roared with laughter. "I *knew* it! I knew you were one of us. Like the freaks always say, 'One of us! One of us!' "

"Yeah, I'm a freak like you," Buffy agreed. "So why are you here? And what has it got to do with Spurs Hardaway?"

"Can't put anything over on you," the old carny said, his eyes lighting up. "Did you know that tonight is the Coyote Moon?" He looked as if he was going to howl in excitement.

"Listen, I don't really care what you do as long as it doesn't harm other people."

Hopscotch frowned. "As a witch, you should know that sometimes you can't avoid that. If we're going to bring Spurs Hardaway back from the dead, we need a blood sacrifice, and lots of it."

"Preferably young and pure," Buffy said.

"Yeah," the old carny agreed. "That's the general

idea. Luckily, you can still find some in a small town like this. It's best when they come of their own free will."

"Okay," Buffy said. "I'll forget I ever heard about this stuff. Just get me out of this box."

"You're lying." Hopscotch sneered. "You won't let us kill a bunch of your friends so we can raise the meanest, evilest skinwalker who ever lived."

"Okay, maybe not," Buffy conceded, thinking furiously. *Now I know their plan for sure.* She suddenly realized that this conversation wasn't an accident—Hopscotch wasn't just lonely for a little company.

"Listen," she said. "Either you're one of those bad guys who likes to brag, or you don't really want Spurs Hardaway raised from the dead."

His voice took on a hard edge. "Do you know what it's like to live for a hundred years in a seedy road show?"

"No. Unless high school counts."

"It's pitiful," the old carny muttered. "No home, no family, no good food, no good mattress, no bathtubs."

"No manicures," Buffy said.

But Hopscotch wasn't finished. "There's nothin' but grease, gas fumes, and ten thousand towns, each one more boring than the last!" He snorted a laugh. "For the ones who have stayed young, there's fun in making whoopee with the locals, but I gave that up a long time ago. I'm a hundred and seventy-five years old!"

"You don't look a day over a hundred," Buffy insisted.

His wrinkled face looked wisftul. "Now the only fun I have is when I put on my skin and run with the pack. Sometimes I think I should just run off and *stay* a coyote. I'm really tired of fixing that stupid Ferris wheel."

"I bet. But won't things get better after Spurs comes back?"

"Not for me."

"Why not?"

" 'Cause I'm the one who shot him dead."

"Oh, bummer," Buffy said. "And he knows this tidbit?"

"He was there."

"Right. Then you might as well get me out of here," Buffy insisted, "because we're partners now."

A look of doubt flashed across Hopscotch's craggy features, and Buffy feared that he would slam the lid on her prison, leaving her to die. Finally, he reached down and hauled her out with strong hands and arms.

When he set her on her feet, she got her first good look at her surroundings. She was in the van area of a large equipment truck, with tools, spools of cable, electronic gear, and other stuff strapped to the walls. She had actually been stored in a large metal tool chest welded to the floor. The grimy tools from the chest were now in a pile at her feet.

The only light came from a naked bulb over their

heads. The only way out was the closed door at the back of the truck, and the old carny stood between her and that door. In his hand was his favorite weapon, a massive wrench that Buffy knew only too well.

"Don't try nothin'," Hopscotch warned.

"I'm still tied up," she said, motioning to her hands behind her back.

"And you're gonna stay that way."

Buffy sat on a spool of electrical cable and stretched her stiff legs. "It must've taken some guts to kill Spurs Hardaway. Why did you do it?"

The old man scowled. "Because we were doing all the work, keeping his Wild West show on the road, and he was taking all the money! He was hardly paying us enough to live on and to feed the livestock.

"I'd been with Spurs since his first rodeo, in 1858, and I didn't want to kill him. But he could be a mean old coot. I always had that silver bullet in my Derringer, just in case he didn't see reason." Hopscotch shook his head sadly. "He didn't see reason." The old man trailed off in thought.

"So how do we stop Spurs from coming back for another curtain call?" Buffy asked, hoping to keep Hopscotch in the present.

Hopscotch smiled. "*We* don't. *You* do."

"Me? Where are you going?"

The old man gave her a crooked grin and opened a red toolbox. Slowly he pulled out a ratty coyote skin and draped it over his shoulders, putting the moth-eaten animal head on top of his own head. Buffy didn't like the way those dried, dead eyes stared down at her.

"I'm not sticking around," Hopscotch vowed. "I'm heading for the hills. If you fail, Spurs will come after me, but I'll lead him a merry chase. If you stop them, you'll break the spell, and we'll all live free. For the first time, we'll have control over our lives."

"But how do I do it?" Buffy asked.

"How do I know? *You're* the witch." He started to unbutton his grimy work shirt, then he stopped. "There is one more thing you should know. Spurs was buried with his grizzly bear skin, and he knows how to use it. He's the only white man I ever seen who could turn himself into a bear. You've got to *be* the animal, and Spurs was a nasty ol' grizzly bear, with supernatural powers."

"Great," Buffy muttered. "Hey, before you go, at least untie me!"

Hopscotch squinted suspiciously at her, then pulled a hunting knife out of his boot. "Turn around."

Buffy didn't like turning her back on the armed carny, but she didn't have much choice. She turned and held her breath. A moment later, she felt the knife slice through the ropes, and her hands swung free.

"Thanks," she said, glancing back at him and massaging her sore wrists.

"You might want to turn around again, unless you don't mind seeing something really weird."

"I've seen weird before."

She had seen weird before, but never quite like this. Hopscotch stripped naked, except for his coyote skin, then from his toolbox he took a bundle of dried leaves all tied together. He struck a match and lit the bundle. In a few seconds, the truck was filled with cloying smoke—Buffy could smell sage and cedar among the pungent odors.

While he sang in a strange language, Hopscotch smudged his body with the burning torch until he looked like a grilled fish. Then the old man got down on his hands and knees and began to writhe to his own silent drums, still singing, sometimes growling. The coyote pelt rode his back like a furry parasite, and Buffy was startled to see the hairs on the pelt start to rise, as if alive. His singing grew more guttural and animal-like.

When she looked back at the man, he was no longer a man, but something in between man and beast. He twitched and growled, and his bones and muscles crackled as they changed shape. The smoke seemed to form around the writhing figure, helping him de-evolve into a wild animal. She could swear that the walls of the truck were glowing as magic filled the small enclosure.

By the time the smoke lifted, a coyote with familiar yellow eyes stood before her.

"Impressive," Buffy said hoarsely. All she could

think about was Spurs Hardaway coming back and morphing into a giant, supernatural grizzly bear.

Acting like a scruffy dog that had just stolen dinner off the table, the coyote padded to the door and waited for her to come over and open it.

"Hmmm," Buffy said, crossing to the back of the semi-trailer. "A skinwalker might make a good boyfriend. When you need a guy, you'd have a guy, and when you didn't want a guy, you'd have a pet."

The coyote snarled at her.

"It was just a joke," Buffy explained. She opened the latch and lifted the door at the back of the truck. The coyote stuck its nose out, sniffed the air, and leaped into the darkness. By the time Buffy looked out the door, it was gone.

The Slayer jumped to the ground and crouched down. She was lucky to be alive, and she knew it. She could easily be dead, if she hadn't run into the only skinwalker who didn't want to see Spurs Hardaway rise from the grave. She couldn't afford to underestimate the gang of shape-shifters again—they were real, and without free will, they were dangerous.

Keeping low and in the shadows, Buffy ran to the vacant lot next door, where most of the cars were parked. She hoped that Giles had followed orders and stayed with his car, because she certainly didn't want to go back into the carnival to look for him.

Be there, Giles! Please be there!

His boring car was there, but he wasn't.

"Giles, you idiot!" Buffy muttered. She looked at

the full moon high in the sky and gulped. It wasn't red, only slightly pink, but Ol' Coyote Moon looked as if she meant business.

Buffy glanced at her watch and saw that it was ten o'clock—she had been unconscious even longer than she thought. There were only two hours left before midnight, and she didn't have a clue where her friends were or how to stop these monsters.

Somewhere a coyote howled, and it sounded as if it was laughing at her.

CHAPTER 8

By ten o'clock, the Saturday night crowd at the carnival was bigger and rowdier than ever, with tons of people laughing, eating, and shrieking. Willow wondered where they had all come from. Maybe the carnies had put up posters in the neighboring towns, too.

She and Xander sat outside a hamburger stand, eating a gigantic plate of greasy french fries and watching the parade along the midway. Whirling rides, bright lights, and blaring music—it was an immortal town, springing up over and over again all over the country. The carnival probably hadn't changed much since Willow's grandparents had gone to it, which was the eeriest thing about it.

With all the frenzied activity designed to mesmerize the senses, Xander still kept looking at his watch.

"Two more hours," Willow said. "And looking at your watch won't make the time go any faster."

"Would it help if I set my watch ahead?" Xander asked, grinning at his own foolishness. "Can you believe it, Willow? It's happening to *us*—a real summer romance!"

Willow sighed. "I'd rather have a romance that lasted summer, fall, winter, and spring." *And happened* between *us,* she thought.

"But that's not a summer romance," Xander insisted. "A summer romance is something special, because it blazes like a comet across the sky and then fades out. The thing that makes it special—that makes everything move so fast—is that a summer romance is doomed to end."

"How poetic. And you don't have to take Rose home to meet your parents," Willow added.

"They wouldn't understand our love," Xander declared, sounding quite tragic.

"Oh, yes they would," Willow said with a laugh. "All too well."

She straightened suddenly. Something in the crowd caught her eye—an older man in a totally unhip cardigan sweater and wool slacks. Before she could get a closer look, he blended into the crowd and was gone.

"What's the matter?" Xander asked.

"I thought I saw Giles."

Xander laughed. "Giles? At a carnival? I don't think he goes out on Saturday night, but if he did go out, it would be to a planetarium or a slide show at the museum. Not to a carnival."

"Yeah, you're right," Willow admitted. "I've been looking for Buffy, but I haven't seen her, either."

"She won't be back, not after the way she embarrassed herself. That girl is just so certain that she's right all the time, she'll never admit it when she's wrong." He laughed and slapped his knee. "What a ditz, thinking these nice people are *werecoyotes!*"

Willow laughed uneasily. "Yes, it is a little silly, isn't it? Say, do you want some ice cream?" She quickly changed the subject.

"Sure." Xander fumbled in his pocket and pulled out a wadded-up dollar bill. "See, I've got some money left."

"That's okay, I've got plenty of money."

"Oh, yeah?" Xander said. "How much?"

"Three hundred dollars."

Xander spit a french fry halfway across the midway. "You've got three hundred dollars? What did you do, pawn your computer?"

"No, I played a little poker with Lonnie, Hopscotch, and the boys. I cleaned them out, as they say. I even paid Lonnie back, with interest."

"Wow! Were they mad at you?"

Willow frowned puzzledly. "No, it was like they didn't care. I have a feeling that they don't really have much use for the money they make here. I mean, what are they going to do with it? They can't own very much stuff, traveling around all the time."

"Yeah, what a romantic life," Xander said blissfully. "It's almost like they're monks—or samurai warriors—on a holy quest."

"And what exactly is that holy quest?"

"To have fun, to bring people pleasure! What higher calling could there be?"

"I suppose," Willow said doubtfully. She wished she were having more fun, and that Buffy were having fun with them. Waiting until midnight to go out on a date with a strange guy from the carnival was not her idea of fun, even if he was a great kisser. With all the money in her bag, she and Xander could have more fun than anybody, if she could just get his attention.

He was looking impatiently at his watch again, and she knew that it was a hopeless cause. How could she compete with somebody like Rose and a summer romance?

Suddenly, she felt strong hands massaging her shoulders, and she turned to see tanned, brawny forearms. She looked up to see Lonnie's smiling face, perfect dimples, and curly blond hair.

"Hi, Lonnie," Xander said cheerfully. "I hear our little Willow cleaned you guys out at poker."

"Yeah," Lonnie said with amusement. "I always knew she had hidden talents."

Willow tried not to blush. "Good cards and money management, that's all. What's the plan for tonight?"

Xander cut in, "I know I'm meeting Rose back at her trailer."

"No, that's changed," Lonnie said. "I talked to

Rose, and we want to double-date with you guys again. We haven't seen much of Sunnydale, so we thought we might do some sightseeing."

Willow didn't know whether to laugh or cry at the crestfallen look on Xander's face. The only sights he wanted to see were on Rose's immediate person.

"That's great!" Willow said, trying not to sound too relieved. "At midnight?"

"We'll try to close early tonight," Lonnie answered. "We'll make an announcement at eleven o'clock to say we're going to close at eleven-thirty. We'll say it's fire marshals or something like that."

"Why close early?" Willow asked.

Lonnie shrugged his perfect shoulders. "We're a little shorthanded. There's been an emergency, and some of our guys were needed elsewhere."

"Was anybody hurt?" Willow asked worriedly.

He stared off into the distance and seemed to be studying the crowd. "Don't worry your pretty little head—we can handle it. You guys just hang out around here, and we'll find you when it's time to go."

"Okay," Willow answered cheerfully. Lonnie waved and wandered off in the direction of his dart booth.

"Nice guy," Xander muttered, "but I'm getting a little tired of double-dating."

"Yeah," Willow said, trying not to show how relieved she was. "I wonder what the emergency is?"

"He said not to worry about it." Xander jumped

to his feet and clapped his hands. "Hey, you've got three hundred dollars! That might even be enough to win a stuffed animal. Want to try?"

"Sure!"

Willow stood up and gazed into the night sky, where a lovely full moon was rising over the merry-go-round. She felt like grabbing Xander's hand, but she knew that would be pushing it. She was content to blend into the fun-loving crowd with him.

Everything is going so well tonight, Willow thought. *Why am I so worried? I can't be concerned about Buffy. If she wants to miss out on all the fun, that's her business.*

"Come on!" Xander said, rushing off toward the games.

"Okay!" Grabbing her bag, Willow hurried after her beloved.

This stinks, Buffy thought as she loitered in a dark corner of the carnival and watched laughing teens tromp past, crunching candy apples and slurping Cokes. Not only were they all having fun, oblivious to the danger around them, but time was slipping away. The Coyote Moon edged higher and higher in the night sky.

Where are you, Giles? She couldn't go out into the bright neon and look for him, as she didn't want the carnies to know she had escaped. She couldn't stay put, because the chances were slim that Giles would just happen to walk past this one spot, between the ticket booth and the Porta Potties. She could stand in another spot, but her chances of finding him wouldn't be any better.

Since his car was still in the parking lot, Buffy reasoned that Giles still had to be here, looking for her. Either that, or he had been captured and stuck in a tool chest, too. That probably hadn't happened, because the carnies had no way of knowing that Giles was with her. They would think he was just a slightly confused parent looking for his wild kids.

She hadn't seen Xander and Willow, either, which had her twice as worried. *I'm never gonna let those two out of my sight again! Whoa, girl!* She caught herself. *Don't take a parental trip!*

She had to do something—but what?

Amid the din of blaring music, clattering rides, and shrieking teens, she heard a gravelly voice. It was the clown on the dunking machine, taunting a customer: "You throw like a girl! In fact, you throw like my *grandmother!*"

Hmmm, Buffy thought.

Keeping to the shadows, she worked her way behind the rides, the food stands, and the game booths. Luckily, the dunking machine was in its own corner of the carnival, removed from the other games because it needed forty feet of throwing room. The redheaded girl was on ball duty instead of Rose, and Buffy wondered where the sleaze queen could be. Was she with Xander?

There's no time to worry about that now, Buffy told herself.

Crouching low, she moved along the fence to the rear of the dunking booth. Most of the flimsy structure was made out of plywood and two-by-fours hammered hastily together, and she had no problem removing a board and slipping under the back wall.

She heard the gravelly voice of the clown—he was making a joke about Sunnydale boys and sheep—and she saw the back of his multicolored fright wig and striped shirt. He looked dry, which was in her favor. Next Buffy located the target disc and the mechanism it tripped. Moving cautiously in the darkness, she ran her hand along the levers and springs until she found the hinge that actually dropped the clown into the water.

He was only a few feet away, just above her. She could smell his earthy, animal odor, and *he* got to take a bath a lot more often than the rest of the carnies. Now that she knew all about the cult of werecoyotes, it was hard to think of any of them as being human. They didn't even smell human anymore.

She waited until he paused in his usual litany of taunts and insults, and then she said quietly, "I want you to announce something."

He put his hand over the microphone, looked down, and growled, "Who's there?"

Still crouching in the shadows, Buffy reached up and shook the platform he was sitting on. "I'll dump you if you call for help."

"Okay, okay! What do you want?"

"Say, 'Librarian, return to your car.'"

"Hey, come on, I'm working here!"

"Do it!" Buffy shook his platform again, and the hinges groaned ominously.

"Okay." The clown removed his hand from the microphone and declared, "Here's a public service announcement. Librarian, you better get back to your car. Pronto."

He looked down and growled, "Happy?"

But Buffy was already gone. She scurried under the loose board, rolled to her feet, and dashed toward the parking lot. Usually, when they faced danger, Giles was a frazzled ball of nerves, certain they were going to get killed at any moment. She had to hope that he was nervously paying attention to everything around him.

When Buffy saw two carnies working on an air compressor dead ahead of her, she pulled out her barrettes and shook up her hair so that it fell in her face. She lowered her head and slipped past them, walking slowly. If they looked at her, she wasn't aware of it, but she listened carefully for voices and running footsteps. When she heard none, she finished her leisurely stroll to the parking lot.

Get your Nikes in gear, Giles! We need to keep ahead of the pack. Buffy paced nervously for a few moments until she saw a familiar figure cutting across the lot. She waved, and he quickened his step.

"Thank goodness," Giles said, clasping her hands. "Are you all right? You look terrible."

"It's the carnival-chic look," Buffy answered, fluffing her stained, ratty hair. "Hey, weren't you supposed to stay by the car?"

"Surely not all night!" Giles protested. "I knew that something had happened to you, and I had to go look. What did happen to you?"

"First something bad, then something good, I think. I found an unexpected ally." She crossed to the other side of the car and waited for him to unlock the passenger door. "Get in, and I'll tell you about it on the way."

"Where are we going?" Giles asked, fumbling for his keys.

Buffy looked warily around the dark parking lot. The flashing lights of the carnival splashed off the hoods of the cars and trucks, twisting into psychedelic shapes. The music seemed distant and tinny, and it felt as if they were alone. But were they? Scrawny canines could be slinking between the oversized tires, stalking them.

"Unlock the car. Hurry!" Buffy ordered.

Giles jumped to attention and opened his car door. He started to get in just as a brown and white coyote bounded onto the roof of the car behind him.

"Duck!" Buffy shouted.

He dove into the driver's seat as Buffy sprang up and slid on her stomach across the roof of the sedan. Fists flying, she smashed into the coyote as it lunged for Giles, and the impact threw them both into the car door next to theirs.

Buffy fell on top of the coyote, which twisted and

squirmed desperately while trying to chomp Buffy's jugular vein. Her crucifix necklace flopped out of her shirt, but it didn't do a bit of good. She had to slug the canine viciously until it was unconscious and limp, something that was repugnant to her. It was so much like a dog!

Buffy jumped to her feet, tossing off the coyote like a smelly fur pelt. She didn't even wait to see what became of it, because she knew that its buds could be nearby, ready to pounce. Buffy scurried to the passenger door, yanked it open, and dove in.

"Drive!" she said breathlessly.

Still shuddering, Giles started the car engine. "Where?"

"The cemetery."

"I was afraid you were going to say that." Looking around carefully, Giles backed the car out of the parking lot. He drove as if he were afraid he was going to run over a coyote wherever he went.

Buffy didn't relax until they were on Main Street, headed back into town. The carnival was far behind them, and it was tempting just to forget about it and hide under the bed. But she couldn't do that, even though she felt out of her element fighting these four-legged Lon Chaneys.

"Why the cemetery?" Giles asked.

"Here's the short version," she began. "I was captured, but I got lucky and got turned over to Hopscotch. Have you seen him? He's the gnarly one. He's also the one who shot Spurs Hardaway."

"Really?" Giles remarked. "So he doesn't want to

see Spurs come back. How much help will he be to us?"

"None. He turned himself into a coyote and took to the hills." Buffy frowned worriedly. "I can't say I blame him. I'm not sure how to stop them, but I know there's one thing we've got to do—get the bear skin."

"A rug?" Giles asked in confusion.

"No, the bear skin that was buried with Spurs Hardaway. We've got to open his coffin and get it out. The last thing Sunnydale needs is an evil sorcerer who can turn himself into a giant supernatural grizzly bear!"

"No, I suppose you're right," Giles said glumly. "And Willow and Xander?"

"I haven't seen them. Have you?"

The Watcher shook his head. "No. But perhaps they stayed home."

"You got a peep at Rose. Do you think Xander would stay home?"

"No, and Willow would stick close to him, if she could."

"She's got her hands full, too," Buffy muttered.

With a grave expression on his face, Giles steered the car onto another quiet suburban street. "We're getting close to the cemetery. What's the plan?"

"We've got to check here first," the Slayer answered, "to make sure they haven't started the masquerade party yet. You stay in the car, while I go scope things out. If it looks clear, we'll get some shovels at my house and steal Spurs's bear skin. To be on the safe side, maybe we can dismember his corpse."

"Silver!" Giles said worriedly. "We've got to get some silver bullets."

"Only as a last resort. I think we can stop them without killing anybody." She opened the car door and slipped out. "You wait in the car—no more rogue warrior stuff. Honk if there's trouble."

"Will do," Giles answered, nervously surveying the quiet street and moonlit cemetery. He quickly locked the car door behind her.

Buffy jogged toward the fence, preparing to leap over the iron spears that surrounded the cemetery. As she was about to go airborne, a horn honked frantically behind her. Buffy pulled up at the last second and crashed noisily into the fence. She turned to yell at Giles, when she saw him pointing frantically down the street.

The Slayer whirled around to see a beautiful Irish setter come charging down the street with three coyotes yapping at its heels. When the frightened dog zigged to either side to escape, the coyotes deftly cut it off and kept it running down the middle. The setter was bigger than the coyotes, and just as fast, but it was obvious from its shiny red coat that it was a house pet, no match for the snarling predators, which would run her down sooner or later.

Buffy saw Giles get out of his car and start waving at the oncoming coyotes and their prey. "Shoo! Shoo!" he yelled.

Once again, it was coyotes behaving badly but

normally. As soon as they saw Giles, they broke off the chase and loped into the shadows, where they watched from a respectful distance. The poor setter ran breathlessly toward Giles, and Buffy moved to head it off.

"Come here, girl," Buffy said, holding her arms out to the frightened animal. The dog lunged gratefully into her embrace, and Buffy rubbed its silky coat. The animal was shivering and panting so badly that it was hyperventilating.

"Oh, you poor girl," Buffy said sympathetically as she kept the three rotten coyotes in view.

"How do you know it's a girl?" Giles asked.

Buffy shrugged. "I don't know, something about her."

"Do you suppose those three are normal coyotes?" Giles asked. "They don't seem as aggressive as the other variety."

"I don't know," Buffy admitted. "We shouldn't take any chances. I thought I told you to stay in the car."

Giles pouted with indignation. "It's difficult to stand by and watch a beautiful animal like that get mauled by coyotes!"

"Yeah, I guess so." Buffy petted the setter's neck, which is when she realized that the dog had no collar or tags. Maybe it had lost its collar during the chase, getting it caught in a fence. A desperate dog could easily squirm out of a collar.

Then Buffy noticed something else—the dog's smell. It was as if it hadn't had a bath in a while. The warning hackles on Buffy's neck were just starting to rise when the dog whirled around with a vicious snarl and chomped her forearm.

"Aaagh!" Buffy screamed, trying to get the dog's powerful jaws to unlock from her arm.

Giles recoiled in horror at the sudden and ferocious attack, and he didn't see the three coyotes as they wheeled on their haunches and charged across the pavement. It was a concerted attack, with two of the coyotes rushing Giles and one coming to aid the dog. Only Buffy had discovered too late that it wasn't a *real* dog.

If they had the right skins, the shape-shifters could turn themselves into any *animal!*

Buffy watched helplessly as two swift coyotes pounced on Giles and drove him to the ground. When the third coyote lunged for her, she lashed out with her free hand and spun it around like a hairy boomerang. But the sweet Irish setter still had her arm in a death grip.

Giles's screams rent the air as the supernatural shape-shifters mauled him!

CHAPTER 9

With a dog that wasn't a dog trying to gnaw her arm off, Buffy got good and mad. She leaned down and bit the setter brutally on its tender snout. With all her might, she tried to chew that weredog's nose off.

When the creature yelped and let go of Buffy's arm, she swung her other fist like a sledgehammer. She crunched the setter on the top of its head, and the beast went limp and slumped to the ground. The Slayer jumped up and booted the unconscious animal about ten feet.

As the setter rolled into the ditch, it took on the momentary appearance of a girl with red hair—Rose's relief at the dunking machine! Somehow the monster shook off the blow and became a harmless-looking dog once again. There was no time to gape at this weirdness, because Giles was still getting mauled.

Two of the attackers were now dazed, but two more were wrestling with the librarian, trying to rip their way through his sweater. Buffy charged across the pavement and flew into them feet-first; the canines went careening twenty feet and landed in a heap. She caught movement from the corner of her eye, and she spun like a top and smacked the first coyote as it tried to sneak up on them.

Crouching protectively over Giles, Buffy kept the four beasts in view. They were dazed and wary, but they knew enough to snarl in anger.

"That was a nice trick you pulled on us!" she said angrily, shaking her fist at them. "I bet if you had a human skin, you could even be human again!"

The canines snapped and snarled at her, but they were cautious now that they had lost the element of surprise. Buffy glanced down at Giles, who was covered in blood but alive. He groaned, rolled over, and picked up his glasses.

"The car!" she ordered. "Get in the car!"

"Gladly," the bloody librarian muttered as he crawled on all fours to the door of his sedan. While the coyotes circled them, Buffy feinted phantom blows at them and Giles hauled himself behind the steering wheel. With a trembling hand, he pulled the door shut.

Glaring at the monsters, the Slayer backed slowly toward the passenger door. She gripped her wounded forearm, which was starting to throb with pain.

"I've had it with you hairballs! I really have!" Buffy warned. "I don't care about the anti-fur movement—I'm going to stitch all of you together into a fur-lined trash bag!"

The coyotes growled bravely at her, but they didn't attack as Buffy slipped into Giles's car. Why should they attack? They had won, driving the intruders away from the cemetery and safeguarding their ceremony. They had used trickery to do it, but that was the way of coyotes.

Giles started the car engine and tromped the gas angrily, sending the coyotes scurrying. He had a lot of scratches and bloodstains on his shirt, but he didn't appear to be badly injured.

"Can you drive?" she asked.

"I'm shaky, but I think so." Giles frowned at the tooth marks on Buffy's arm. "We should go to the hospital. We probably both need stitches."

She gulped. "We're not going to, like, turn into werecoyotes, are we?"

Slowly the car pulled away from the curb, and Giles shook his head. "No, this isn't a curse, like the typical werewolf account. These people studied and worked hard to become shape-shifters, and they've had more than a hundred years of practice."

Buffy turned to look for the werecoyotes and the weresetter, but they had disappeared into the dark landscape of the cemetery. She gazed into the sky and tried to find the moon, but it was too high overhead—the roof of the car blocked it. *Just as well,* Buffy thought. Exhausted, she slumped into her seat and tried to ignore the throbbing pain in her arm.

"I know a doctor who could patch us up," Giles said. "That way, we won't get bogged down in red tape at the hospital."

"Good thing, because we've got to get back to the carnival by midnight," Buffy said, gritting her teeth. "We need to head off Willow, Xander, and whoever else they have on a leash. Maybe *you* can talk some sense into them. Hopscotch said they had to come of their own free will."

"Which they're doing." Giles shook his head with frustration. "Our foe is crafty and dangerous, and they know *you're* the only one who can stop them."

"So what else is new?" Buffy asked with a shrug. "What's spooky is, when they're animals, they act like real coyotes. When they're in that wild state, we should be smarter than them."

"You mean, they should have some weakness we could exploit?"

"Yeah. We need to start using trickery, too, or the next mayor of Sunnydale is going to be a werebear."

Giles nodded gravely and kept driving through the deserted streets, while the skull-colored Coyote Moon beamed down on them.

"Due to a request from the fire marshal, the carnival will be closing in five minutes!" a voice announced on the loudspeaker. Willow looked up, recognizing Lonnie's drawl. There were groans from the paying customers all around her, who were not done partying. Although it was twenty-five after eleven, the midway still boasted a sizable crowd.

"If you have any ride tickets left, come back and use them tomorrow!" the friendly voice suggested. "The rides and games will shut down in five minutes. Good night, and thanks for coming!" With a crackle of static, his voice cut off, and the surfer music cut in.

"At last!" Xander grinned with delirious happiness, as he hugged the gigantic stuffed tiger he had won. Willow knew that it wasn't a tiger he imagined he was hugging—it was a Rose. She tried to keep the jovial smile plastered to her face, but it was hard.

Having fun at breakneck speed, they had returned to the carnies almost sixty dollars of the poker money she had won. But it was worth it for the good time they'd had, playing the games, riding the rides, and eating too much junk. If only life could be this simple—just she and Xander out on a date, acting like a regular couple. Why did they need Lonnie and Rose?

For one brief, shining moment, Willow wondered if she could whisk Xander away, before Rose showed up to turn him into Silly Putty.

"Xander," she said hesitantly. "What if Buffy is right, and there is something wrong with these people?"

He smiled pleasantly at her. "Hey, Willow, you know what? If you're getting cold feet and want to back out, go ahead. You've got enough money to call a cab." Xander reached into his pocket, fished around, and pulled out a quarter. "Hey, I'll even call the cab for you!"

Willow tried not to pout. "You want me to go, so you won't have to double-date."

"Bingo. I like Lonnie, but we don't need him, either. Rose and I can party by ourselves, if you know what I mean."

Willow cleared her throat. "Has it ever occurred to you that this summer romance might come with certain trade-offs? I mean, nothing else is *free* at this carnival."

A momentary look of concern passed over Xander's face, and he tried to hide it with a nervous chuckle. "Now, what could you be thinking of?"

"Come on," she insisted, "spill it. What's it going to cost you?"

Xander rubbed his jaw thoughtfully. "Let me ask you something, and I want you to give me an honest answer. Where do you think is a good place for a guy to have a tattoo?"

Willow frowned. *First a mustache, then a tattoo? Can a Harley be far behind?* She gestured with her hands as she tried to improvise an answer. "Someplace nobody would see it. Maybe on your . . . around your . . . on the bottom of your foot!"

"Ow!" Xander groaned at the very thought. "What we do for love."

Willow sighed and looked around at the hubbub

of excited teenagers trying to catch a last thrill before the vacation ended. Those who hadn't come with dates were pairing up, or trying their best to pair up. Cliques of boys and girls had suddenly become smaller and tighter.

She looked at Xander, thinking that the hardest part of the evening was still ahead of them, when she would have to watch him and Rose paw each other. She would also have to be pawed by Lonnie, while Xander was nearby, which was confusing and strangely titillating. But it still seemed wrong, as if there was a scam she hadn't figured out yet.

Willow lowered her voice, which was hardly necessary in the crush of carnival-goers. "You know, Buffy has supreme gut instincts. What if she's right—what if there really is something wrong—"

"The only thing wrong with Rose is that she's leaving too soon," Xander sighed, dewy-eyed.

"I'm serious."

Xander smirked. "Hey, I think it's great to have Buffy jealous of *us,* for once. I think it's good for her to be cut down to size. I notice that she had enough sense to stay away from the carnival tonight and not make a fool of herself anymore. If we're in such danger, where has Buffy been all night?"

"I don't know," Willow admitted. "I guess there was nothing to it."

Xander suddenly sprang to his feet and waved frantically. "Over here!"

With a corn dog revolving slowly in her stomach,

Willow turned around and got even sicker. Rose came strolling toward them, wearing a tight leopard-patterned dress, fishnet hose, and spiked heels. Men's heads swiveled, and their eyes followed her like the wake of an ocean liner. She was carrying a very large clasped purse—maybe it contained her bowling ball.

"Why don't you get your tattoo on your forehead?" Willow suggested.

"Good idea," Xander said, not even hearing her. He was totally oblivious to everything but Rose, who sauntered toward them in slow motion.

When she got closer, Xander slammed the stuffed tiger into Willow's arms to make room for the stuffed carny. "You look beautiful!" he gushed.

He tried to wrap his arms around her, but she teasingly pushed him away. "My public is watching. There will be time later."

Willow swallowed hard. "Your dress is . . . stunning."

"Thank you," Rose anwered. "I got this outfit in a burlesque house in Abilene."

"Beautiful," Xander repeated.

"They still have burlesque houses in Abilene?" Willow asked puzzledly. "I thought that burlesque houses went out of fashion in the 1950s."

Rose gave a throaty chuckle. "It's not really active, more like a burlesque museum."

"You mean, some old stripper used to wear that outfit?" Xander asked, obviously impressed.

Rose smiled. "You might say that."

"Where are we going?" Willow asked cheerfully, desperate to change the subject.

"I don't know," the carny replied. "Let's wait and see what Lonnie wants to do. He's the one who has the pickup truck. Xander, poor baby, you might have to ride in the back, in the bed of the truck."

"No problem," Xander said bravely. "If I get any boo-boos, will you kiss them and make them feel better?"

"Yes, my baby," she cooed, patting his cheek.

The corn dog wanted to escape from Willow's stomach, just as she wanted to escape from Rose, but neither one got the wish. It was clear that Xander would go anywhere with Rose, even if he were tied to a chain and being dragged by the truck.

"So you want to see the sights of Sunnydale?" Xander said, tapping his chin thoughtfully. "That could be a pretty short trip. There's the Bronze, which is a cool club, even though they let everybody in. Then there's a crummy mall, one lone coffee shop, and the slot-car races—they might still be open. And we have the usual collection of historical sights."

"Historical sights," Rose said, lifting a dark eyebrow mysteriously. "I've always gotten turned on by old places."

"Really?" Xander said excitedly. "There are some ancient ruins on Flagpole Hill—probably *cavemen* left them."

"It's an old army depot," Willow corrected him. "From World War Two."

"That was a long time ago," Rose said wistfully. She gazed up at the moon that was high overhead. "But it won't be much longer."

Before Willow could question that odd statement, the colorful lights on the Octopus blinked off, and the Ferris wheel creaked to a stop. One by one, the mammoth machines of the midway stopped spinning and went dark. The rock music faded out, and the speakers blared nothing but static. Even the calliope on the merry-go-round went silent. Lights on the poles stayed lit to help people find their way out, but the carnival was dying down.

"Thanks for coming, everybody!" Lonnie said over the loudspeaker. "We'll be open every day from six P.M. until midnight. Come back and see us!"

For the first time that night, it was quiet in the carnival as the customers picked up their posters, stuffed animals, and dates and began to file out. Several of them waved to Rose, who waved back. *In this strange, fake town,* Willow thought, *Rose really is a celebrity.* When the carnival closed, it was almost as if she had no identity, unless she wore a stripper's costume from the 1950s.

Although the carnies were cute, Buffy was right—they were *weird.*

Willow was suddenly struck by an irrational burst of fear and guilt, and she felt like running for the exits along with the other customers. But she looked at Xander making goo-goo eyes at Rose, and she realized that he would need protection. For one thing, if he came home with a grotesque tattoo, he would probably be grounded for months.

She heard cheerful whistling, and she turned to see Lonnie striding toward them. He was also dressed for going out on the town—carny-style—with a white cowboy hat, fancy rodeo shirt, silver belt buckle, clean jeans, and shiny cowboy boots. In his hand was a grimy duffel bag. Willow wondered if he thought they were going to a square dance, or maybe the gym.

"Lonnie, my man!" Xander said, trying to sound like one of the gang. He had almost perfected the carny slouch, but it would be years before he could grow the facial hair. Every time Willow saw Lonnie, he looked hairier, which was also distressing.

He put his arm possessively around her slim waist. "Hey, are we ready to party, or what?"

"We were just trying to decide where to go," Rose said. "Xander mentioned some historical sights."

"The truth is, our historical sights aren't too exciting," Xander explained. "Unless old cannons really turn you on."

Lonnie laughed. "Sometimes they do."

"What's in the bag?" Willow asked nonchalantly.

He hefted the old duffel bag. "Just something to make the party even more lively. I'll show you later."

"You know what I like?" Rose asked with a twinkle in her dark eyes. "Cemeteries."

Xander laughed nervously. "Is that right? Cemeteries, huh?"

"I hear this town has a really cool old cemetery," Lonnie said.

Willow piped in, "How about the old courthouse? It's a classic example of Greek Revivalism."

Lonnie turned to her, his blue eyes piercing hers. "After the cemetery, okay? We're the guests, right?"

"Right!" Xander said, shooting a warning glance at Willow. "The cemetery is dark and quiet—fine with me!"

Are you forgetting about the last time we were in that cemetery? Willow wanted to scream. But she said nothing. After all, Lonnie and Rose couldn't be vampires, as they were up all day like regular people. They drank root beer, not blood.

"The truck's this way," Lonnie offered, steering the slender girl between the dark fun house and the boarded-up ticket booth. "Xander and your stuffed tiger will have to sit in back. You can sit up front with me."

"Okay," she said meekly. Willow really wanted to run for the hills and escape this weird double date, but Lonnie had her firmly in his grasp. Behind her, Rose giggled, and she turned to see the carny and Xander nuzzling each other as they walked.

It wouldn't be nice to break the date now, she rationalized. *There are too many other people involved.*

Despite her fears, Willow followed Lonnie through the deepening shadows behind the false fronts. Twenty feet ahead of them loomed a beat-up pickup truck, and she was about to climb into it and go to a cemetery with an itinerant laborer who worked at a carnival. At least they would be in a familiar neighborhood, and Xander would be along.

This date isn't hopelessly insane, is it?

As they neared the truck, Willow gazed at Lonnie in his white cowboy hat, and he gave her the double-dimple smile. She sure hoped he was the good guy he appeared to be.

In a small office on the first floor of a charming two-story house, a kindly country doctor still practiced medicine. The white-haired physician put on the last pieces of tape over a butterfly bandage that covered a cut too shallow to stitch. Then he covered Buffy's entire forearm with a protective sheath of gauze and taped it down.

Dr. Henshaw smiled wearily. "That will hold for tonight, but you'll have to come back tomorrow to have the bandage changed."

"Okay," she promised, glancing nervously at the watch on her opposite wrist.

"And be careful," the doctor warned. "No physical exertion, or you could rip out the stitches. That goes for you, too, Giles."

The librarian nodded gravely. He had a protective bandage stretched across his chest, where he had received most of his wounds. He grimaced in pain as he pulled on an old flannel shirt the doctor had loaned him.

"Those tetanus shots could also make you drowsy," Dr. Henshaw said. "Better go home to bed. You know, in forty years of medical practice in this town, I've seen some strange things, but I've never seen anyone who had coyote bites."

"We were in the wrong place at the wrong time," Buffy said with a helpless shrug. "We tried to save a dog from being attacked—dumb thing to do."

"Yes," Giles said, buttoning his shirt. "Thank you, Dr. Henshaw, for seeing us at this late hour."

The old country doctor stood and stretched. "Think nothing of it, Giles. You've helped me so many times to find obscure journals and pamphlets." He turned to Buffy and explained, "I have an interest in holistic turn-of-the-century medical cures, and Giles is a font of knowledge."

"Isn't he, though?" Buffy agreed, jumping to her feet. "Thanks a lot, Dr. Henshaw, but we've got to get going. Past my bedtime, you know."

The doctor escorted them to the front door. "Take a painkiller to keep the swelling down. Remember, I want to see both of you tomorrow."

"Believe me, we'll be very happy to be around tomorrow," Buffy assured him.

"Yes, indeed," Giles agreed. "Until tomorrow."

They hurried out the door and down the steps. Buffy felt a little woozy from all the medicine, but she tried not to think about it. With a final wave to the doctor, they jumped into Giles's car, and he started the engine.

"You've got to take me home," Buffy said as she settled into her seat.

"Are you done for the evening?" the Watcher asked in horror.

"Not yet. I feel burnt-out, but I'm hanging in there. I need to go home and get a weapon."

Giles squealed the tires pulling away from the curb. "What kind of weapon would you have at home?"

"A werecoyote weapon," she muttered. "And you've got to find something that will work against them, too. Our usual bag of tricks—stakes, holy water, crucifixes—doesn't do click. And don't tell me you're going to plug them all with silver bullets. Our friends will be hanging with them, and we're not going to turn this into a summer action movie."

"I've been racking my brain, trying to think of something," Giles said as he tooled down the quiet tree-lined street. "There is one possibility. I've never told you this, but I used to raise hounds—for the fox hunt."

"But of course."

"At home, I have a high-pitched dog whistle, the kind that humans can't hear. I wonder if it would work on coyotes . . ."

"Who knows? It's worth a try. With this whistle, you could call them over from someplace else, right?"

"Theoretically, they would come to the whistle blower. But coyotes are unpredictable." Giles slowed down to take a corner.

"But if any of them were human, they couldn't

hear it and wouldn't know what was going on." Buffy pointed. "My house is coming up."

"I know. Please be quick getting your secret weapon." Giles coasted to a stop in front of her middle-class abode, which looked dark and slumbering this close to midnight.

Buffy slipped out the car door and shut it quietly behind her. She padded up to the front door, got out her key, and let herself in. Luckily, her secret weapon was in the dining room, which was near the front of the house. If her mom heard her at all, she would simply think she was coming home. *Knowing Mom, she'll save the lecture for tomorrow.*

Less than a minute later, Buffy got back into the car. She was wearing a clean jacket and hiding something underneath it.

"Let me see," Giles said eagerly.

Buffy grinned and held up an elegant silver carving knife with an S engraved on the handle. "I always knew the sterling silverware would be good for something."

Giles frowned worriedly. "You'll have to get awfully close to them to use that."

"Every time I see these coyotes, I get close to them. We're like a deodorant commercial."

"Next stop, my house," Giles said, twisting the steering wheel.

Five minutes later, the librarian came running out of his tiny bungalow, clutching a brass whistle which hung from a chain around his neck.

He jumped into the car, panting for breath. "I

actually looked for silver bullets, but I couldn't find any. Remind me to order some."

"From the Monster's End catalog, right?" Buffy asked. She looked grimly at her watch. "We can still get to the carnival by midnight. Go to warp drive."

The Watcher slammed his car into gear and sped away from the house. After a few minutes of rather swift driving for Giles, they roared up to the vacant lot that was hosting the carnival. There were lights—but only a few—and only a handful of cars were parked on the lonely country road. None of the rides was running, and the place was deserted except for a few stragglers. In the dark, the odd towers, structures, and wires looked like some kind of alien prison.

"What's the deal?" Buffy asked, jumping out of the car. She looked at her watch. "What time have you got?"

"Five minutes before midnight." Giles also got out of the car and stared in disbelief at the silent machines and dark booths. Two hours ago, this ghost town had been bursting with screams, music, and teenage hormones. Now it was dim and drained of life, like a corpse.

She saw some kids hanging out at an old convertible, just watching the stars, and she yelled over to them, "What happened? Did this place close early?"

"Yeah, at eleven-thirty!" one of them hollered back. "Stupid fire marshals."

"Oh, man!" Buffy muttered. "They're alone with Xander, Willow, and those other lovesick fools."

"Thank you!" Giles called politely to the kids in the convertible. "Are there any people still working here?"

"I think most of them left, too."

Buffy gazed upward and saw the Coyote Moon hanging high in the black sky, glowing like a Japanese paper lantern. The face on it seemed to be laughing at her.

Chapter 10

Just what they needed after gorging themselves on junk food all day was some more junk food, so Lonnie drove the rusty pickup truck to the Dairy Queen. Even though Willow was flush with money, Lonnie insisted on paying. Armed with swirled and dipped cones, the rambunctious double-daters headed for the cemetery, with Willow sitting in the front seat between Lonnie and Rose.

Thanks to aged shock absorbers, Xander was bounced pretty hard in the bed of the truck. But he had the stuffed tiger for padding.

Willow had to admit that she felt better after the stop for ice cream, even though her overworked stomach balked at processing it. Getting ice cream was just so wholesome that it made up for going to the cemetery. She noticed that Lonnie didn't eat much of his dessert, either.

His duffel bag sat between Willow's feet, and she was sorely tempted to unzip the zipper and look inside. From what she could tell by poking at it with her toes, the bag contained clothes, or maybe a blanket. *Yes, a blanket probably would be part of the proceedings.* Willow licked gingerly at her ice cream.

On the other side of her, Rose devoured everything, including the sugar cone.

"Hungry?" Willow asked.

"Always," Rose purred. As if a curious thought had just occurred to her, she looked appraisingly at Willow. "You know, you could be half cute, if you would develop some style."

"Other people have told me that," Willow said. "My friend Buffy—"

"Grrrr," Lonnie growled under his breath.

"Pardon me?"

"Nothing," Lonnie said. "Just clearing my throat. Say, is this where we turn?"

Willow nodded. "Yes. You seem to know your way around Sunnydale pretty well."

"You bet," Lonnie answered with a laconic grin. "I saw it all when I was putting up posters and passing out handbills. Do you know the best way to get into the cemetery?"

"You can usually squeeze through the gate, if it's even locked," Willow answered with a knowing grin. *Or, if you're a Slayer, you can just jump over.* "It's the third drive on the right, behind those trees."

As the headlights of the truck sliced through the hedges around the cemetery gates, Willow saw several other cars and trucks parked in the street. "That's funny, there are other cars parked here."

"Maybe other people had the same idea," Lonnie muttered.

"Somebody's probably having a party," Rose suggested. "See, that house across the street is all lit up."

"Yeah, that's probably it," Willow agreed. "Are you sure you want to do this—it's not too late to see the courthouse."

Lonnie chuckled and turned off the engine. "I'm sure. How's your ice cream?"

"Great," she lied.

"Good." Lonnie grabbed his bag at her feet, opened the door, and stepped out. Warm, flower-scented air flowed into the truck cab.

Rose patted Willow's hand reassuringly. "Don't worry, honey, we won't bite. Much."

Grabbing her oversized purse, she oozed out of the car and held her hands out to Xander. "Hey, baby, we ready to party?"

"You bet!" He crawled over the stuffed tiger and vaulted out of the truck into her arms. They kissed disgustingly for several seconds, until Rose shoved him away and sauntered toward the gate. Xander loped after her like a puppy.

Willow was frozen in the truck, knowing that she had a chance to back out but only if she took it right now. *Why the cemetery? Whatever happened to parking on lonely country roads?*

Lonnie stuck his head in the window, and Willow

jumped. "It's such a beautiful night," he drawled. "Come out and sit with us for a while. Howl at the moon."

Willow laughed nervously. "It's just my stomach—it's a little upset from all the junk food."

"I promise I won't feed you anything." Lonnie smiled charmingly.

"Okay, for a little while." Willow opened the door and stepped out.

With Rose in the lead, the foursome walked up to the wrought-iron gate, which was already open a crack. The padlocked chain that normally held it shut was nowhere to be seen.

"Oh, they stayed open just for us," Rose said with amusement. The gate creaked open as she pushed her body against it. Xander stumbled after her, his libido totally in charge.

"This looks like an old cemetery," Lonnie said, his hand warm and active on Willow's back, massaging her fears away. "Is anybody famous buried here?"

She thought about that question as she strolled through the gate. "There was Herbert Jeremiah, who invented the bathing cap, and I think there was some old rodeo cowboy. Many of the town's founding fathers are buried here. You know, Sunnydale is a lot older than it looks."

"I'm sure of that," Lonnie said, shutting the gate behind them. "That rodeo cowboy—where might his grave be?"

"Well, if he was really famous, he's down in the hollow, where the mausoleums are." Willow tried not to shiver as she surveyed the bleak landscape of tombstones, gnarly trees, and little mansions for dead people. *And undead,* she thought, remembering the last time she and Xander had been lured to the mausoleums by dates. At least there was plenty of light, with the full moon casting a silvery glow over the spooky proceedings.

She looked for Xander and Rose and saw them on the fresh-cut lawn, wrestling playfully. As they tussled and rolled about, they looked more like two puppies than two lovers, and Willow hoped that Rose thought of Xander as a younger brother. In the next instant, that hope was dashed as the wrestling degenerated into a lip-lock and embrace—right there in the cemetery, under a full moon.

Lonnie's hand tightened around her waist, and she let herself be dragged along the sidewalk. Despite his amorous clinch, he seemed to be in a hurry to get deeper into the cemetery—and to keep her close. Willow gazed back at Xander and Rose, who were still writhing in the dew. If she ignored reality in favor of fantasy, she could insert herself into Rose's place. But she would still prefer someplace dry.

Without warning, the petite carny tossed Xander off as easily as if he were a bedsheet. He rolled about twenty feet down a hill and crashed into a tombstone, while Rose jumped to her feet, laughing.

She was fixing her dress as she walked past Lonnie and Willow. "He's a frisky one, all right. Let's go see that big white spire down there."

Willow broke away from Lonnie to see if Xander was all right, but he came loping toward them. From the goofy expression on his lipstick-smeared face, she could tell that he was still lobotomized.

"Wow!" was all he could say as he staggered past them.

Angry and sad, Willow had a sudden urge to kiss Lonnie in front of Xander, and her face must have broadcast that loud and clear. Lonnie hovered closer, and she sensed that earthy, animal smell about him. Before she had a chance to meet his tender lips, Willow wrinkled her nose and sneezed!

"Sorry," she said with a sniffle. "I must be allergic to something. I don't understand it—I'm usually only allergic to dogs."

Anger flashed on Lonnie's handsome features, then he tipped his hat back and was once again charming. "Lots of stuff growing around here, especially ragweed. Let's catch up with them, okay?"

As long as Lonnie was being a gentleman, Willow wasn't going to be frantic about this strange site for their date. In many respects, it was better to be with a gentleman than a raving maniac like Xander. Their behavior wasn't all Rose's doing—it took *two* to mosh.

A fleeting shape caught her attention before it vanished behind a tree trunk. It was too low to the ground to be human—it had to be a dog or some other kind of animal. *Maybe that's why I sneezed.* Willow hoped it wasn't a skunk. She watched the tree, but she didn't see any other sign of movement.

Then she heard voices, and they weren't coming from Xander and Rose, who were only a few feet ahead of them. The voices were coming from down in the hollow, where mausoleums and fancy tombstones decorated the city of the dead.

Rose had mentioned a white spire, and there not only was one, but about ten people were milling around it. At first, this was reassuring to Willow, because they were obviously living people. But the more she thought about it, the stranger it seemed that they would go to a cemetery at midnight and find a bunch of people already there. Once again, she told herself that the carnies couldn't be vampires. They lived in the sun; they ate corn dogs.

"You weren't kidding," Xander said puzzledly. "There really is a party here."

As they strolled toward the gathering, Willow realized that half of these other people were carnies and the other half were local kids. They were all on a mass double-date!

She turned to Lonnie and asked, "What's going on?"

"It's just something we do in every town," Lonnie said with a shrug. "We don't know if there'll be a decent club or a park, but every town has a cemetery. So we just have a party there one night after work."

"You could've told us," Xander muttered. If anything, he was more disappointed about seeing all these people than Willow was. She hoped that he would go home disappointed.

"Oh, lighten up," Rose said, running a red-lacquered fingernail under Xander's chin. "The more, the merrier."

Doing a quick count, Willow saw there were exactly seven carnies and seven local kids, counting the four of them. Among the carnies was the red-haired woman and the dark-haired guy she had whipped at poker. Apparently, the old guy, Hop-scotch, had not been able to get a date.

The carnies sat about on the tombstones with studied indifference, while the local kids looked awkward and confused. Whatever they had expected to happen this night, it wasn't hanging around in a cemetery, staring at one another. But as long as Xander's plans were upset, too, Willow wasn't going to complain too loudly.

"What do we do now?" she asked. "Charades? Kevin Bacon?"

"We'd like to put on a little show for all of you," Lonnie announced. He nodded to his fellow carnies, and they climbed down from their perches and formed a rough line in front of the grave under the white spire. All of them were carrying some kind of bag or purse, and one of them lit a bundle of dried leaves. A pungent, spicy smoke filled the dark hollow in the cemetery.

Willow and Xander drifted closer to each other.

From the side of his mouth, Xander whispered, "I hope they're not going to try to scare us."

"They already have," Willow answered. "I'm ready to bolt when you are."

"Let's see what happens."

"A hundred years ago," Lonnie began somberly, "a great man lived in this town. His name was Spurs Hardaway, and this is his grave. He was a showman, like us. In fact, you might say he was our inspiration and guiding light."

Lonnie exchanged a confident look with his fellow showmen. "Spurs enjoyed all types of sports; best of all, he loved to hunt. In honor of Spurs and his favorite pastime, we do a little show that we call the Coyote Dance. Tonight we have the perfect audience and the perfect moon gazing down upon us. Let us begin with a song."

Willow wouldn't exactly call it singing—not those strange whoops, cries, and guttural groans. The carnies looked properly spooky as they swayed and twitched in the silvery moonlight, surrounded by tombstones. All of the local kids were now bunching together, as if they were on the opposite team, waiting for a kickoff.

"Well, their singing bites," Xander murmured, "and their dancing is not much better."

"I'm ready to go when you are."

As the smoke from the flaming torch swirled around them, the carnies began to remove their clothes. It wasn't a sensual striptease—just people ditching their clothes, as if they were about to take a shower.

Xander grinned at Willow. "Hold on, things are looking up!"

A few other kids giggled, but the possessed performers paid no attention to them. They continued stripping, singing, and swaying—as if no one in the whole world were watching them. That was the most disturbing part of their act. Just when Willow thought things couldn't get any weirder, they reached into their duffel bags and pulled out old coyote skins, which they draped over their shoulders.

Xander looked at her and shrugged. "Costumes."

"This is too weird," Willow said. "I'm outta here."

She started to walk away from the twitching carnies, with two more local girls right behind her. Before they got ten feet, they were stopped short by the sound of low growls. The three girls stared in horror as half a dozen coyotes leaped upon tombstones and paths, cutting off their escape.

She heard gasps and shouts from the others, and she whirled around to see the seven dancers down on their hands and knees, trembling and growling as if possessed. The smoke swirled around them, making them look as if they were changing shape. As Willow stared more intently, she realized they *were* changing shape.

They were morphing into coyotes!

Triumphant howls echoed all around them, as the coyotes cut loose in unison. She now realized that they were surrounded by at least fifteen coyotes. That didn't even count the ones writhing on the ground, turning *into* coyotes.

His eyes wide with fright, Xander sidled closer to Willow. "Next time, I'll listen to Buffy."

"Been there, thought that," she admitted.

A deep groaning sound came from behind them, and Xander, Willow, and the teens whirled around to see the grave under the white spire start to shudder. The earth and withered flowers crumbled away, as if an earthquake had gripped that grave and no other. They heard splintering noises—as if the coffin under the soil was also breaking apart.

Suddenly, several coyotes attacked the grave and began to dig furiously, trying to free whatever was in there. Trembling, Willow lifted her eyes to read the name on the grave: "Spurs Hardaway."

Some of the other teens tried to make a break for it, and they were instantly surrounded by vicious coyotes. Snapping and growling, the canines herded them back into a frightened huddle. When one boy didn't move fast enough, a dark brown coyote lunged and bit his calf. Shrieking, he hobbled after the others. The number of coyotes had doubled, and Lonnie and his friends were . . . gone.

Everywhere Willow looked, there was something horrible going on, especially behind her. Thanks to the frantic digging of the coyotes, the grave was open, and something was pounding its way out of its coffin. Chunks of rotted wood flew outward, and skeletal fists reached toward the sky.

"Release me!" groaned a low voice that wasn't remotely human.

From the full moon overhead came a bright beam of light, which struck the sphere at the top of the white spire. It exploded as if hit by lightning, and sparks and debris flew everywhere. Willow ducked to the ground, and she was sorry she did, because now she had a level view of the open grave.

She gaped as a grotesque, worm-eaten corpse rose slowly from the pit. The monster was wrapped in a ragged bear skin, complete with rotted head. Smoke, leaves, and wind swirled all around this gruesome apparition as he threw his skull back and cackled.

"Ladies and gentlemen, it's good to be back!"

The coyotes howled and yipped triumphantly, while the teens whimpered in terror.

"Okay, guys," Xander said, backing away from the zombie astride the grave. "You scared us—that was really . . . something! Can we leave now?"

The coyotes seemed to laugh, and the gruesome corpse spoke in a hollow voice. "Not yet. You haven't seen my best trick."

Crunching like a pile of bones, the monster slumped forward and was completely covered by the ratty bear skin. The mangy pelt looked a million years old. As the coyotes yipped and yowled and the teens wept, the old bear skin swayed back and forth. Lightning crackled in the sky, and the moon turned a horrid shade of red.

Willow blinked because she couldn't believe her

eyes. Black hairs on the back of the pelt began to rise and twitch. *Must be static electricity,* she thought.

Xander gripped her hand, frightened. "It's all our parents' fault for moving to the Hellmouth."

"I know," Willow said.

For some reason, the coyotes stopped howling, and they began to look around, puzzled. A few of them even loped off toward the street, and the others trailed after them, uncertain what to do. The terrified local kids seized the moment and ran like jackrabbits in the opposite direction. Willow was about to do the same when she heard a roar that was so thundering it shook the trees to their roots.

She whirled around to see an enormous grizzly bear rearing over her and Xander. It had to be at least ten feet tall—a thousand pounds of teeth, gristle, and muscle! The primeval monster roared again, sounding furious and very, very hungry.

"Say no to fur!" a voice shouted.

Willow and Xander flopped to the ground as a lithe figure came bounding through the air behind them. It was Buffy! Doing gymnastic flips, the Slayer flew over their heads and smashed into the chest of the grizzly bear. The beast roared in outrage and staggered backward, clawing at something shiny in its fur.

Willow realized that Buffy had stabbed it with some kind of sword—she could only see about two inches of the handle. With a loud grunt, the Slayer hurled herself into the grizzly one more time, knocking it back another ten feet. The bear's enormous bulk smashed into the white spire with such force that the whole thing teetered, crumbled, and fell. Tons of white marble came thundering down around the wounded animal.

Buffy rolled away at the last moment as the entire monument imploded into the earth. The bear's anguished growls became strangled human cries—then nothing at all—as chunks of marble crushed the creature. After a few moments, a haze of dust and a sickly stench of death rose from the grave, but nothing else.

Xander instantly turned to Buffy. "Hey, we believed you the whole time! We were just keeping an eye on them, because you were, like, nowhere to be seen."

"Thanks," Willow said. She didn't have enough breath left to say more than that, but she really meant it.

Buffy sighed. "I hope my mom doesn't check the sterling silver." She snapped her fingers. "Giles!"

The three of them jogged across the cemetery and out the main entrance. In the street, they found Giles sitting in his car, with about twenty coyotes clawing at the vehicle. He had his window down a crack and was blowing on something—but making no sound.

He saw them, and Buffy waved. A moment later, Giles started up his engine and drove off slowly, with the coyotes bounding playfully behind him.

"Too bad," Buffy said. "I think your dates have dumped you—for a guy with a dog whistle."

"Why be *coyotes?*" Xander asked, totally confused. "Isn't it fun enough being humans? Especially when you look like *that?*"

Buffy shook her head. "It's a long story. Let's get a good night's sleep and meet tomorrow morning. We can all go together to see them. Now that they don't have a leader, maybe we can talk some sense into them."

"Will you walk us home, Buffy?" Willow asked.

The Slayer smiled and put her arm around her friend's shoulder. "Sure. Was he at least a good kisser?"

"Yeah." Willow grinned.

AFTERWORD

Buffy, Willow, Xander, and Giles drove out to the vacant lot about noon the next day, but they were too late. The carnival was gone—every bolt, compressor, and stuffed animal. In the spot where the Ferris wheel had stood the day before, there was nothing but the ashes and dying embers of a large bonfire.

When they stopped to poke around the fire, they noticed the charred remains of several animal skins. That seemed to have been the purpose of the fire—to burn the skins.

"Hopscotch said that the spell would be broken if we stopped Spurs Hardaway from coming back," Buffy remarked. "Maybe now they're free to live their own lives."

"Human lives, let's hope," Giles added.

"I hope they find peace," Willow said.

Buffy felt eyes gazing at her back, and she turned to see a lone coyote standing high on the hill behind the vacant lot. She waved at the old coyote, and it turned and loped away.

About the Author

John Vornholt has had several writing and performing careers, ranging from being a stuntman to writing animated cartoons, but he enjoys writing books most of all. He likes playing one-on-one with the reader. John has written over a dozen *Star Trek* books, plus novels set in such diverse universes as *Babylon 5* and *Alex Mack.* His fantasy novel about Aesop, *The Fabulist,* is being adapted as a musical for the stage.

John presently lives in Arizona with his wife, Nancy, and their two kids, Sarah and Eric, and he goes roller-skating three times a week. He used to see a lot of coyotes in the hills of Hollywood, where he lived for seventeen years, and he often sees them now in the Sonoran Desert. Keep your eyes open, and you may see one, too.

Send e-mail to John at: jbv@azstarnet.com

"Well, we could grind our enemies into powder with a sledgehammer, but gosh, we did that last night."

— XANDER

As long as there have been vampires, there has been the Slayer. One girl in all the world, to find them where they gather and to stop the spread of their evil ... the swell of their numbers.

#1 THE HARVEST

#2 HALLOWEEN RAIN

#3 COYOTE MOON

#4 NIGHT OF THE LIVING RERUN

THE ANGEL CHRONICLES, VOL. 1

BLOODED

THE WATCHER'S GUIDE
(The Totally Pointy Guide for the Ultimate Fan!)

Based on the hit TV series created by Joss Whedon

Published by Pocket Books

1399-06